"What exactly is it you suspect me of, Mr. Kinross?"

Rebecca's face was flushed.

"You're angry with me, and quite rightly." Brod dropped his hand off the rail and stood straight. Another foot and their bodies would be brushing. "From where I'm standing I think you might be trying to steal my father's heart."

It was a mystery to Rebecca how she kept her cool. "All I'm asking, Brod, is you give me the benefit of the doubt before starting to label me 'adventuress.'"

"Most women can't resist being the object of desire."

She felt as if they were engaged in some ritual dance, circling, circling. "That's something I know nothing about." Her simmering temper was making her eyes sparkle.

"Quite impossible, Rebecca." His lips curved. "If you put on your dowdiest dress and cut off that waterfall of hair men would still want you."

She had the disturbing sensation Brod had reached out and touched her. Run his fingers over her skin.

Dear Reader,

Ever since I can remember, our legendary Outback has had an almost mystical grip on me. The cattlemen have become cultural heroes, figures of romance, excitement and adventure. These tough, dynamic, sometimes dangerous men carved out their destinies in this new world of Australia as they drove deeper and deeper into the uncompromising Wild Heart with its extremes of stark grandeur and bleached cruelty.

The type of man I like to write about is a unique and definable breed—rugged, masculine and full of vigor. This Outback man is strong yet sensitive, courageous enough to battle all the odds in order to claim the woman of his dreams.

A *Wife at Kimbara* is the first of three linked books where I explore the friendships, loves, rivalries and reconciliations between two great Australian pioneering families. They are truly LEGENDS OF THE OUTBACK.

Margaret Way

Margaret Way

Look for:
The Bridesmaid's Wedding #3607 June 2000 ✓
The English Bride #3619 September 2000

A Wife at Kimbara
Margaret Way

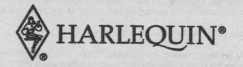

TORONTO • NEW YORK • LONDON
AMSTERDAM • PARIS • SYDNEY • HAMBURG
STOCKHOLM • ATHENS • TOKYO • MILAN • MADRID
PRAGUE • WARSAW • BUDAPEST • AUCKLAND

ISBN 0-373-03595-0

A WIFE AT KIMBARA

First North American Publication 2000.

CHAPTER ONE

BROD strode from the blinding light of the compound into the welcoming gloom of the old homestead's hallway. His whole body was sheened with sweat and his denim shirt covered in dust and grass stains. He and his men had been up since dawn driving a herd of uncooperative cattle from drying Egret Creek to Three Moons, a chain of billabongs some miles off.

It had been a long hot slog filled with plenty of curses and frustration as several beasts in turn tried to break away from the herd. Dumber than dumb in some situations cattle had a decided ability to hold their own in the bush.

He could do with a good scrub but there was scant time for that. His schedule was as hectic as ever. He'd almost forgotten, the station vet was flying in this afternoon to give another section of the herd a general check over. That was about three o'clock. He had time to grab a sandwich and a cup of tea and return to the holding yard they'd set up under the gum trees.

Now he focused on the stack of mail neatly piled on top of the rough pine bench that served as a console. No Kimbara this he thought with bleak humour. Definitely not the splendid historic homestead of his birth.

His father resided on Kimbara. Stewart Kinross. Lord of the Desert. Leaving his only son to slave his guts out running the cattle chain while he claimed all the glory.

Not that there weren't quite a few people in the know.
Not that it bothered him all that much he thought swiv-
elling to throw his black Akubra onto a peg on the wall.
It landed unerringly on the target as it always did but
he paid no attention. His day would come. He and Ally
together had quite a stake in the diverse Kinross enterprises with ancestral Kimbara, the flagship of the
Kinross cattle empire the jewel in the crown.

Grandad Kinross, legendary hero, had seen to that,
never blind to his son Stewart's true nature. Andrew
Kinross was long gone while his grandson lived a near
outcast on Marlu for the past five years. In fact it had
been since Alison, hiding her heartache over the
breakup of her passionate romance with Rafe Cameron,
left home for the Big Smoke, the name the Outback
bestowed on big bustling cosmopolitan Sydney.

Alison said then she wanted to try her hand at acting
like their celebrated Aunt Fee who had taken off at
eighteen full of wild dreams of making a brilliant career
for herself on the London stage. And wonder of won-
ders Fee had actually succeeded despite a well publi-
cised out of control love life. Now she was back on
Kimbara writing her sensational memoirs.

Fee was quite a character, too famous to qualify for
black sheep of the family but with two big-time broken
marriages behind her and the legacy of an exquisite
English rose of a daughter. Lady Francesca de Lyle, no
less. His and Ally's cousin and from what they'd seen
of her as good as she was beautiful. Couldn't have been
easy with the arty oversexed Fee for a mother.

Now Fee was telling all, convinced her biography
would be a huge success in the hands of one Rebecca
Hunt, an award-winning young journalist from Sydney

with another well received biography of a retired Australian diva under her belt.

Just to think of Rebecca Hunt lit a dangerous flame somewhere inside him. Such was the power of a woman's beauty he thought disgustedly when he distrusted her like hell. He had no difficulty summoning up her image. Satiny black hair framing a lily cool face, but with one hell of a seductive mouth. The mouth was a dead give-away. Yet she was so utterly immaculate and self-possessed she was darn near mysterious. He could never imagine someone like him for instance mussing that sleek hair or laying a finger on her magnolia flesh. She was way too perfect for him. Brod gave an involuntary laugh the fall of light in the hall giving his lean handsome features a brooding hawklike quality. In reality the patrician Miss Hunt was just another mightily ambitious woman.

It wasn't his father that had her in thrall. No way would he accept that. Not that his father wasn't a big handsome guy, assured, cultivated, filthy rich, fifty-five and looking a good ten years younger. Forget the meanness there. No it was the wild splendour of Kimbara that interested Miss Hunt, of the large ravishing grey eyes. Eyes like the still crystal waters of a hidden rock pool, yet he had divined instantly Miss Hunt would discard her promising little career any day to become mistress of Kimbara. From a fledgling career to riches beyond her imaginings. Only one catch: She could only have it all while his father lived. After that it was his turn.

The Kinross tradition had never been broken. Kimbara, the Kinross's ancestral home was passed directly from father to firstborn son. No one had ever abdicated in favour of a brother though Andrew Kinross had been a second son, surviving the Second World War when his elder brother James hadn't. James had died in his brother's arms in a far distant desert, very different from their own. One of the countless terrible tragedies of war.

Shaking his head sadly, Brod moved to pick up the mail riffling through it. It had been flown in that day while he was far out on the run. Wally his loyal, part aboriginal ex-stockman had brought it up. Since he had badly smashed his leg in a fall from his horse, Wally's duties revolved around the small homestead and the homestead's vegetable garden, which was currently thriving. Wally wasn't turning into a bad cook, either. At any rate better than him.

Only one piece of correspondence really caught his eye and somehow he had been expecting it. He ripped it open smiling grimly at the contents. Why would the old man contact him directly when he was so good at letters? He took a harsh breath. No "Dear Brod." Nothing like that. No enquires as to his health. It appeared his father had arranged a gala event to impress and entertain Miss Hunt. A polo weekend at the end of the month. In other words ten days' time. Matches starting Saturday morning with the main event 3:00 p.m. Usual gala ball in the Great Hall Saturday night.

His father would naturally captain the main team, read, hand-pick the best players. His son Brod would be allowed to captain the other. His father hated like hell that his son was so damned good if a bit on the wild side. God pity him, his father seemed to hate everything he did even as the chain thrived. If the truth be known his father didn't look on him as a son at all. Since he had grown to manhood his father had treated him more like a rival. An enemy at the gate. It was all so bloody bizarre. Small wonder he and Ally were emotionally scarred, but both of them had confronted it.

Their mother had run off when he was only nine and Ally a vulnerable little four-year-old. How could she have done it? Not that he and Ally didn't come to understand it in time. Getting to know their father so well, his black moods, the colossal arrogance, the coldness and the biting tongue they reckoned their mother had been driven to it. Maybe she would have fought for their custody as she swore she would but then she had gotten herself killed in a car smash less than a year later. He vividly remembered the day his father had called him into his study to tell him about the accident.

"No one gets away from me," Stewart Kinross had said with a chilling smile on his face.

That was Brod's father.

He shook his head in despair. At least he and Ally, the closest of siblings, had had Grandfather Kinross to turn to. For a while. A finer man had never been born. The best thing that had ever been said to him had come from one of his grandfather's closest friends, Sir Jock McTavish.

"You have all your Granddaddy's great fighting heart and spirit, Broderick. I know you're going to live up to the legend!"

Jock McTavish knew how to size a man up. In the many shattering confrontations Brod had had with his father over the years he tried to hold fast to Sir Jock's words. It hadn't been easy when his father had never ceased trying to grind him down.

Brod sighed and thrust his father's letter into the pocket of his jeans. He had no desire to travel so far, he told himself. It was one hell of an overland trek from Marlu to the Kinross stronghold in the Channel Country in the far south west of the giant state of Queensland. Plus he was too damned busy. If he went at all he would have to fly. His father sure hadn't offered to pick him up in the Beech Baron. He'd have to call up the Camerons as he did frequently even after Ally's breakup with Rafe.

He'd grown up with the Cameron brothers, Rafe and Grant. The history of the Kinross and Cameron families was the history of the Outback. It was their Scottish ancestors themselves, close friends from childhood who had pioneered the fabled region in the process turning themselves into cattle barons. Both dynasties had survived. Not only survived, flourished.

Sudden frustration seized him. He remembered as vividly as yesterday the time Ally had come to tell him she couldn't marry Rafe. She was going away. A journey of self-discovery she called it. Her romance with Rafe was simply too overwhelming for comfort.

"But hell, Ally, you love him!" He could hear his own disbelieving voice. "And he sure as hell is crazy about you."

"I love him with every breath that's in me," Ally had responded passionately, fiercely wiping tears from her face. "But you don't know what it's like, Brod. All the girls fall for you, but not a one of them has touched your heart. Rafe squeezes the heart out of me, do you see? I'm sick of him and sick with him. He's more than I can take on."

Bewildered he had ploughed on. "So he's forceful? A man's man. He's not in the least like our father. There's nothing dark and frightening about Rafe, if that's what you're worried about. He's one hell of a guy. What's got into you, Ally? Rafe is my best friend. The Kinross'es and the Camerons are damned near related. We all thought your marriage to Rafe would finally unite our two families. Even the old man is all for it going ahead. Marvellous choice and all that. Couldn't be more suitable.'' He aped his father's deep, polished tones.

"I can't do it, Brod," Ally had insisted. "Not yet. I have to learn a lot more about myself before I take on Rafe. I'm terribly sorry to disappoint you. Father will be furious." Her beautiful clear green eyes darkened at the prospect.

He had taken her in his arms then, hugging her to him. "You could never disappoint me, Ally," he told her. "My love for you is too great. My respect for your wisdom and spirit. Maybe its because you're so young. Barely twenty. You have your whole life in front of you. Go with my blessing but for God's sake come back to Rafe."

"If he'll have me." Ally had tried to smile through her tears.

It hadn't happened. Rafe had never seriously been drawn to another woman but the one person they never talked about was Alison. That subject was taboo. Tough, self-sufficient as he was giving no sign of hurting, Brod knew. Ally had dealt his friend a near mortal blow.

Momentarily disconsolate he stared sightless through the open doorway. Five years later and Ally still hadn't returned home. Ally like Fee had developed quite a talent for acting. Something in the genes. Ally had just won a Logie for best actress in a TV series drama playing a young doctor in a country town. She was enormously popular for her beauty and charm, the way she gave such life and conviction to her frequently affecting

role. He was full of admiration for her but he really missed her; the comfort and humour of her company.
God knows how Rafe, being Rafe, coped with the bitterness of rejection that must have accumulated in his heart? He didn't take it out on him though Grant, the younger brother had been known to fire off a few salvos. Rafe and Grant were as close as he and Ally. To hurt one was to hurt the other. Both brothers would be certain starters in the main polo match the coming Saturday afternoon. Both excellent players though Rafe had the edge. But neither was going to faze him.

He liked the going tough and dangerous and he didn't think he'd have too much trouble persuading one or both to join his team despite his father and he'd need their help getting to Kimbara.

The Cameron's historic station Opal Plains bordered Kimbara on its north-northeast border. Grant ran a helicopter service from Opal that covered their part of Outback while Rafe was master of the vast station. Aristocrats of the Outback, the press called all three of them. They presented a polished front to the world, but there had been plenty of sadness and tragedy in their lives.

No, even if he could cadge a ride with Rafe and Grant he had no desire to confront either his father or the magnolia skinned Rebecca. If the truth be told he couldn't bear to see them together. His father showing that seemingly flawless young woman all the exquisite care and consideration he had never accorded his daughter, let alone his wife.

Often to amuse as much as torment himself he conjured up the ridiculous picture of Stewart Kinross down on his knees before the luminous eyed Miss Hunt begging for her hand in marriage. His father so rich and powerful he thought he was invincible. So sure of his virility, he thought he possessed such sexual magnetism he could easily attract a woman half his age. If it weren't so damned likely it would be funny. Women couldn't resist power and money. Especially not adventuresses.

He'd have to find out a little bit more about Miss Rebecca Hunt, he decided. She was remarkably close lipped about her past though he knew from the blurb on the back of the recent biography she'd been born in Sydney in 1973. That made her twenty-seven. Three years younger than he. The rest went on to list the not inconsiderable achievements of her short career.

She had been named Young Journalist of the year at the age of twenty-four. She'd worked with the Australian Broadcasting Commission, SBS and Channel 9. Two years with the British Press. A book of interviews with the rich and famous. The diva's biography. Now Aunt Fee.

Next to nothing about her private life, though. It might have been as blank as a nun's only Miss Rebecca Hunt behind the cool facade was so absolutely fascinating she couldn't have escaped at least a few sexual encounters. If she was footloose it had to be by choice. Was she waiting for the right man? Charming, clever, rich and powerful.

Most people thought Stewart Kinross was just that, until little bits of him occasionally seeped out. The ego, the self-centeredness, the caustic tongue. But when he set out to, Brod had to admit, his father could be dazzling. A young woman like Miss Rebecca Hunt was bound to be socially ambitious. If she took on his father she would get more than she bargained for, the conniving little witch. He almost felt a stab of pity.

No, he didn't want to go, he told himself, suddenly realising he wanted to go very much.

CHAPTER TWO

REBECCA was standing on the upstairs balcony looking out over Kimbara's magnificent home gardens when Stewart Kinross finally tracked her down, as purposefully as a hunter tracks his quarry.

"Ah, there you are, my dear," he smiled indulgently, as he moved to join her at the balustrade. "A bit of news I thought you might like to hear."

She swung to face him, so lovely he couldn't take his eyes off her.

"Then let's hear it!" Rebecca responded brightly, shying away from the thought her host had taken quite a fancy to her. A thought too embarrassing to pursue. For all his wealth, suavity and charm, Stewart Kinross was of an age with her father. Not that a man as rich and handsome as that couldn't get just about any woman he wanted. But not *her*. Involvement, even with a man her own age wasn't an option. Peace of body, mind and heart were too important. Yet Stewart Kinross was looking at her delightedly out of grey-green eyes.

"I've organised one of my famous polo weekends for your enjoyment," he told her, realising she was making him feel younger with every passing day. "The Matches will be followed by a gala ball, Saturday night with a big breakfast cum brunch in the garden Sunday morning through to noon. After that our guests like to get off home. Most fly, some make the overland trek.

"It sounds exciting." Rebecca struggled a little to sound enthusiastic. In truth her heart was thumping

14

though none of her disquiet showed in her face. "I've never actually attended a polo match."

"Why do you think I've organised this weekend?" he chuffed, his handsome mouth curving beneath a full, beautifully clipped moustache. "I overheard you telling Fee."

She felt a sudden loss of safety. Stewart Kinross for all his charm was a man who was used to getting what he wanted. It would be a disaster if he wanted something from her she couldn't possibly provide. "You're very kind to me, Stewart," she managed to say. "You *and* Fiona," she stressed. "I do appreciate it."

"You're very easy to be kind to, my dear." He tried to keep the feeling out of his voice but failed. "And you're making Fee so happy with what you're doing with her book."

"Fee has a fascinating story to tell." Rebecca turned slightly away from him, leaning her slender body against the white wrought-iron balustrade. "She knows everyone who's anyone in the English theatre as well as so many powerful international figures. There's just so much subject matter. An abundance of it."

"Fee has lived a full life," he agreed somewhat dryly. "She's a born actress as is my daughter, Alison." His voice was surprisingly cool for a proud father.

"Yes, I've seen her many times on television," Rebecca said admiringly. "Some of the episodes have been remarkably affecting because of the wonderful quality of her acting. She brings her character, the country doctor, to such life. I'd love to meet her."

"I don't think you'll see Alison back here." He sighed with evident regret. "She's well and truly settled in Sydney. She rarely comes home on a visit. Then, I sometimes think, it's only to see Brod not the father she's almost forgotten.''

Rebecca looked at him more sympathetically.

"How can that be? I'm sure she misses you. Being the star of a top rating television series must put a lot of pressure on her. I imagine she has very little free time.''

"Alison was raised in the Outback," Stewart Kinross said his expression judgemental. "On Kimbara which if I say so myself is a magnificent inheritance. She has no need to work.''

"You can't mean you'd deny her a career?'' Rebecca was taken aback.

"Of course not.'' He took his cue from her tone. "But Alison made a lot of people unhappy when she left. Not the least the man who loved and trusted her. Rafe Cameron.''

"Ah the Camerons.'' Rebecca remembered all the stories she'd heard. "I researched their family history at the same time I was researching yours. Two great pioneering families. Legends of the Outback.''

He accepted her accolade as though she were speaking directly about him. "Our families have always been very close. It was my dearest wish Alison would marry Rafe. A splendid young man. But she chose an acting career just like Fee. I'm telling you because you'll be meeting Rafe at the polo. I've scheduled it for the weekend after next.

"Rafe will never forgive, never forget what Alison did to him and even as Alison's father I don't blame him. Rafe is Brod's best friend, I think a good steadying influence on him. Brod is a rebel, which you might have gathered. Has been since his childhood. A pity because it makes for a lot of friction between us.''

"I'm sorry," Rebecca responded. "Will he be coming for your weekend?"

"He's certainly been invited." Stewart Kinross looked away over her head. "But Brod likes to keep me begging. The thing is he's needed to captain the opposing team. At least he inherited his prowess from me. I expect I'll hear from him at his leisure. I'm very keen for this to go well, Rebecca. I want you to enjoy your time out here as much as possible."

"It's wonderful to be here, Stewart," Rebecca said, her heart sinking at the look in his eyes.

"What would you say to a ride this afternoon." He put his hand on her arm leading her back into the house lest she escape him.

"That would be lovely, Stewart," she responded, careful to inject a note of regret, "but Fiona has need of me. We're really moving along with the book."

He bowed his handsome head powerfully, protectively over her. "My dear, you can't refuse me. I can do some persuading when I have to. I'll set it straight with Fee and you and I can take the horses out. It's wonderful you ride so well. I want you to look on your time with us as part work part vacation."

"Thank you, Stewart," Rebecca murmured, feeling trapped and somehow ungrateful as well. Stewart Kinross had been the kindest and most considerate of hosts. Perhaps her early experiences had left her a bit paranoid.

In the early evening Broderick Kinross rang. As it happened Rebecca was passing through the hallway so she backtracked to answer the call.

"Kinross homestead."

Whoever was at the other end said nothing for a moment then a male voice so vibrant, so unforgettable, it gave her a shock responded. "Miss Hunt, I presume."

"That's right." She felt proud of her calmness.

"Brod Kinross here."

As if she didn't know. "How are you, Mr. Kinross?"

"Just wonderful and such a tonic to hear your voice."

"I expect you want to speak to your father," she said quickly, feeling the sharp edge to the black velvet delivery.

"I expect he's enjoying his pre-dinner drink," he drawled. "No, don't disturb him, Miss Hunt. Instead could you please tell him I'll be at Kimbara...."

Not *home?* She listened.

"For the polo weekend. Grant Cameron is giving me a lift should my father decide to send the Beech for me. Dad's pretty devoted you know."

Sarcasm without a doubt. "I'll tell him, Mr. Kinross."

"I trust in time you'll be able to call me Brod." Again the ghost of mockery.

"My friends call me Rebecca," Rebecca finally said.

"It suits you beautifully."

"Why must you sound mocking?" She brought it out into the open.

"That's very good, Miss Hunt." He applauded. "You know how to pick up nuances."

A sparkle of anger lit Rebecca's eyes. She was glad he couldn't see it. "Let's say I know how to pick up warning signals."

"Quite sure of that?" he responded just as coolly.

"You don't have to tell me you don't like me." He could scarcely deny it after that first time.

"Why in the world wouldn't I," he answered and rang off with nothing resolved.

What *was* he getting at? Rebecca let out a short pent-up breath, replacing the receiver rather shakily. Their one and only meeting had been brief but disturbing. She remembered it vividly. It was late last month and he had flown in to Kimbara unexpectedly...

She had put on her large straw hat before venturing out into the heat of the day. Fee had had a slight headache so they had taken a break. Every chance she had she liked to explore this fantastic environment that was Kimbara. The sculptural effects of the trees, the shrubs and rocks, the undulating red dunes on the station's south-southwestern borders. It truly was another world, the distances so immense, the light so dazzling, the colours more sun-seared than anywhere else. She loved all the burnt ochres the deep purples the glowing violets and amethysts, the grape-blues that made such a wonderful contrast to the fiery terracottas.

Stewart had promised her a trip into the desert when the worst of the heat was over and she was greatly looking forward to it. It would be too much to expect she would be granted the privilege of seeing the wild heart burst into bloom. No rains had fallen for many long months but she had seen Stewart's collection of magnificent photographs of Kimbara under a brilliant carpet of wildflowers and marvelled at the phenomenon. Not that localised rain was even needed to make the desert bloom, he had told her. Once the floods started in the tropical far north sending waters coursing southward, thousands of square miles of the Channel Country could be irrigated. Swollen streams ran fifty miles across the plains they were so flat. It was such a fascinating land

and a fascinating life. Stewart Kinross had to live like a feudal lord within his desert stronghold.

She had just reached the stables complex, which housed some wonderful horses, when she heard the clash of voices. Men's voices not dissimilar in timbre and tone. Angry voices that made her go quiet.

"I'm not here to take orders from you," Stewart Kinross was saying in a rasping voice.

"That's exactly what you're going to do unless you want to scuttle the whole project," the other younger voice answered none too deferentially. "Face it, Dad, not everyone likes the way you operate. Jack Knowles for one and we need Jack if this enterprise is going to succeed."

"That's *your* gut feeling is it?" There was such a sneer in it Rebecca recoiled.

"You should have some," Stewart Kinross's son quipped, sounding to Rebecca's ears convincingly tough.

"Don't lecture me," his father came back thunderously. "Your day is not yet and don't you forget it."

"Not with you on about it all the time," the son retorted. "An argument, Dad. That's the best reward I ever get. But hell, I no longer care. In case you've forgotten I do most of the work while you sit around enjoying the benefits."

At that Stewart Kinross exploded but Rebecca waited for no more. She turned abruptly shocked by the palpable bitterness of the exchange. She had heard Stewart Kinross and his son weren't close but she hadn't been prepared for the depth of that disaffection. She had heard as well Broderick Kinross at the age of thirty ran the Kinross cattle empire from distant Marlu. Something he seemed to have confirmed. It was all very disturbing.

Even as an outsider she felt the emnity. It was a new insight into Stewart Kinross as well. Fee had assured her her nephew and niece, Brod and Alison, were wonderful young people. Not that Fee had seen a great deal of them with a life based in London. But she spoke of them both with great affection.

It occurred to Rebecca for the first time, though Fee was a great talker, she was remarkably reticent about her only brother. Certainly Rebecca felt appalled by the cold venom of Stewart Kinross's tone. She would have thought he would be immensely proud of his son.

Troubled by what she had overheard Rebecca walked quickly away. The last thing she wanted was to be seen but her efforts were doomed to failure. Both men must have moved off in her direction because a few moments later Stewart Kinross's commanding voice required her to stop.

"Rebecca," he called in a nice mix of authoritarian and genial host.

She turned watching them emerge from the stables complex, probably on their way back to the house.

"Stewart!" Even with her large shady hat she had to put a hand to her eyes against the brilliant sunlight.

Two men in silhouette. Both very tall, a couple of inches over six feet, one with the full substance of maturity, the other a whipcord rangy young man, both wearing the standard Akubra, the younger man with a decidedly rakish tilt. He had a great walk, she thought, putting her in mind of some actor, a kind of graceful lope.

She felt little tears in her eyes at the near unendurable light and wondered why she hadn't brought her sunglasses.

They caught up with her easily and she had her first

sight of Broderick Kinross, heir to the Kinross cattle and business empire.

She didn't know how she had pictured him. Handsome certainly, given the family good looks but not *this*. He literally blazed. The blue eyes so vivid they trapped her gaze. For an instant she had the extraordinary sensation something had cut off her breath.

"Rebecca, may I introduce my son, Broderick." Stewart Kinross looked down at her, sounding as though he preferred not to. "He's here for an interim report to me." He continued more briskly. "Brod, this is the very clever young woman who is writing Fee's biography as I'm sure you've heard. Rebecca Hunt."

Rebecca gave Broderick Kinross her hand perturbed by the adrenaline that was pouring into her body. She looked up into a lean, striking face, beautiful glittering blue eyes. For someone who had laboured long and hard to maintain a fail-safe cool facade she now felt bathed in heat.

"How do you do, Miss Hunt." He was perfectly courteous, on the formal side, yet she felt the shock and hostility that was in him. Why? "When I last spoke to Fee she was very happy with the start you've made on the book. Obviously she has confidence in you."

"I'm very grateful that she thought of me at all," Rebecca said, subdued by the tingling in her hand. "I'm not terribly well-known."

"Don't be so modest, my dear," Stewart Kinross responded in a voice like warmed syrup. He draped a proprietorial arm around her shoulder. Something he had never done before. "I read your biography and thoroughly enjoyed it." Very gently he turned her around, enchanted by the way the large straw brim of her hat shadowed her face. "You really shouldn't go wandering around in the heat. For all that charming hat you risk burning that lovely skin.''

Why the hell don't you hug her, Brod thought with black humour.

He never thought he would live to see adoration in his father's eyes, but this was coming mighty close. Fee had confided to him on the side ''your father is quite taken with Rebecca.'' More like infatuated.

Brod felt a bit shell-shocked himself and he'd had more than his share of girlfriends.

She was lovely in a way that didn't appeal to him at all. The hot-house flower. Good bones, but delicate like a dancer. A little scrap of a thing. No more than five-three. Big light-filled grey eyes, satin near-black hair that fell almost to her shoulders and curved in under her chin and that fabulous skin. All the girls he knew had a golden tan, were tall and athletic and they didn't wear beautiful silly hats with brims that dipped and flowers and ribbons for a trim. Miss Rebecca Hunt was no wildflower. She was an exotic. A vision of cool beauty.

''I take it we've finished our business for the day, Brod.'' Stewart Kinross turned his handsome head with its immaculate cream Akubra to address his son.

Brod took his eyes off Miss Hunt for a moment to answer. ''Please, Dad, give me a break. I can't go away without speaking to Fee.'' The words were said with gentle irony, but Rebecca could see he had no intention of going.

''Well then, come along,'' Stewart Kinross answered pleasantly, but with a certain glint in his eye. ''I'm sure Mrs Matthews—'' he referred to Kimbara's long time housekeeper ''—can provide you with some after-noon tea.''

"So have you had sufficient time to form an opinion about our world, Miss Hunt?" Brod asked, falling back into line with the petite Miss Hunt in the middle. He was glad his father had at last removed his arm from her delicate shoulders. He felt like flinging it off himself.

"I love it." Her charming voice was filled with sincerity. "It may seem strange but I don't know my own country as well as I know some places overseas."

"There is the fact Australia is so big," he offered dryly, indicating the vastness around them.

"And you can't be all that long out of university?" He glanced down at her meaningfully.

"I'm twenty-seven." She gave him a shimmering cool glance.

"My dear, in that hat you look seventeen," Stewart Kinross complimented her.

"Scarlet O'Hara," Broderick Kinross murmured, sounding none too impressed. "You didn't once travel Outback?"

"As I say, oddly no." Rebecca gathered her defences around her. "My work kept me in Sydney for the most part. I spent two wonderful years overseas, based in London, though I never got to meet Fee. I've visited all the state capitals, tropical North Queensland many times. I love it. I've holidayed on the Great Barrier Reef, but this is another world after the lushness of the coastline. Almost surreal with the vast, empty landscape, the monolithic rocks, and the extraordinary changing colours. Stewart is going to take me on a trip out into the desert."

"Really?" Broderick Kinross shot a glance at his father, his cleanly cut mouth compressed. "When is this?"

"When the worst of the heat dies down a little," Stewart Kinross said with almost a bluster.

"Magnolias wilt in the heat," Broderick Kinross lowered his head to peer at the curve of Rebecca's cheek.

"Trust me, Mr. Kinross." Rebecca's head shot up as she gave the sardonic Broderick a brief sidelong glance. "I don't wilt."

"I'm holding my breath until you tell me more about yourself," he retorted, a faint catch of laughter in his voice. "I'm sure any young woman as beautiful as yourself has a boyfriend somewhere."

"Actually, no." She wanted to cry out, "Please leave me alone." He was getting to her as he obviously meant to.

"What is this, Brod, an interrogation?" his father asked, drawing his thick black eyebrows together.

"Not at all. If it seemed like that I apologise," he said. "I'm always interested in your visitors, Dad. Miss Hunt seems more interesting than most."

Interesting wasn't the word. A true femme fatale.

They had just reached the main gate of the compound, a massive wrought-iron affair that fronted the surrounding white-washed walls when a nesting magpie shot out of a tree, diving so low over their heads Rebecca gave an involuntary cry. She was well aware magpies could be a menace when they thought the nest was under threat. The bird wheeled with incredible speed clearly on the attack but this time Broderick Kinross, with a muffled exclamation, pulled her against him with one arm and made a swipe at the offending bird with his black Akubra.

"Go on, get!" he cried, with the voice of authority. The bird did, keeping just out of range.

To Rebecca's searing shame her whole body reacted to being clamped to his. It was a dreadful weakness that she thought long buried.

"It can't hurt you." He released her almost immediately, staring up at the peacock-blue sky. "They're a damned nuisance when they're nesting."

"You're all right aren't you, Rebecca?" Stewart Kinross asked, genuinely solicitous. "You've gone rather pale."

"It was nothing, nothing," she began to laugh the moment off. "It's not my first magpie attack."

"And you've told us you're pretty brave." Broderick Kinross caught her gaze. A moment that spun out too long.

"I told you I don't wilt," she corrected, a tiny blue pulse beating in her throat.

"No." A ripple of something like sexuality moved like a breeze across his face. "Wasn't she magnificent, Dad?" he teased.

"You must understand that Broderick likes a little joke, Rebecca," Stewart Kinross said, a crack appearing in his grand manner.

"Then I generously forgive him," Rebecca spoke sweetly even though her breath still shook in her chest.

What she wanted out of life was peace. That she intended to guard fiercely even against a cyclonic force. Broderick Kinross had the dark, dangerous power to sweep a woman away.

On the Saturday morning of the polo match, Fee woke late, still feeling weary from insufficient sleep. She turned on her back easing the satin pads from her eyes. Living so long in England she had all but forgotten the brilliant light of her homeland. Now she had these eye pads on hand for the moment when the all powerful sun threw golden fingers of light across the wide verandah and into her bedroom.

She was a chronic insomniac these days. Nothing seemed to cure it. She'd tried knock out pills—get up in the morning and have a good strong cup of coffee advice from her doctor—but she hated drugs, preferring herbal cures, or relaxation techniques, not that she had ever been a great one to relax. Too much adrenaline in the blood. Too many late, late nights. Too many lovers. Too many after performance parties. Too many social events crammed into her calendar. She thought she might be able to unwind once she returned home but it wasn't happening.

Of course she and Stewart never did get on, as children and adolescents. Stewart so absolutely full of himself. Since birth. Fiona had taken herself out of the jarring environment of playing second fiddle to her swaggering brother, The Heir, by setting sail for England. Of course her beloved dad, Sir Andy, shocked out of his mind at the prospect of losing his little princess had tried to stop her but in the end when faced with her shrieking virago acts sent her off with enough money to keep her in great style while she studied drama in preparation for her brilliant career. She'd managed this through a combination of beauty—let's face it, even at sixty she could still make heads swivel—lots of luck, the Kinross self-confidence and a good resonant speaking voice, possibly from all that yelling outdoors. She had the lung capacity to fill a theatre like her good friend La Stupenda. And the Gods be praised, native talent. If you didn't have that you had nothing.

The thing that was really niggling away at her was this new potentially destructive situation with Stewart and Rebecca. God knows she'd seen enough of ageing men wearing pretty things young enough to be their daughters even granddaughters on their sleeves, but she wasn't at all happy about Stewart's interest in this particular young woman she'd become so fond of. Apart from the big age difference, part of her wanted badly to warn Rebecca against her brother's practised charm. How could any young person, a near stranger, know what lay beneath the superbly self-assured manner? No wonder little Lucille, her dead sister-in-law had run off. Lucille so gentle a spirit would have fared badly trying to withstand Stewart's harsh nature. In the end she'd shrunk from it.

And there was the way Stewart had treated his children, especially Broderick, who had his mother's glorious eyes although he was clearly a Kinross. Sir Andy had written to her often about his concerns and she had seen for herself Stewart's coldness towards his children whenever she returned home. Those were the years when her darling Sir Andy was still alive. She wouldn't be here now much as she loved the place of her birth only for the fact Stewart was trying to talk her into selling her shares in several Kinross enterprises. There were many family interests to discuss. No need for her to run off. This was the home of her ancestors.

Oddly enough it had been Stewart who had begun all the talk about her writing her biography. He had even suggested a possible candidate for the job. A young award-winning journalist called Rebecca Hunt, already the author of a successful biography about another family friend, opera singer Judy Thomas. *Dame* Judy lest any of us forget. Stewart had read Judy's autographed book and been impressed. He'd also seen the young

Hunt woman being interviewed on one of those Sunday afternoon programs about the Arts.

"Ask her out here, Fee," Stewart had urged her, laying a compelling hand on her shoulder. "If only to see if the two of you could get along. After all, my dear, you've had a dazzling career. You have something to *say*."

She'd fallen for it hook, line and sinker, closing her eyes to the past, gratified by his interest, thinking Stewart could be very charming now that he'd mellowed. Clever, clever, Stewart.

She'd done what he wanted. Lured Rebecca into his trap. Stewart had obviously fallen in love with her. On sight. She was just the sort of patrician creature he had always liked with her pure face and haunted eyes. Oh, yes, they were haunted for all Stewart thought they were cool as lakes. Rebecca had a past. Behind the immaculate exterior, Fee suspected Rebecca had her own story to tell. A story involving some very bitter experience. One that lay hidden but not buried. Fee knew all about the wilderness of love.

She threw back the silk coverlet, putting her still pretty bare feet to the floor. Much as she adored the company of her nephew, secretly revelled in watching him outplay his father in all departments on the polo field, she just knew this weekend was going to bring plenty of tension and heartache.

Why had Stewart invited Brod in the first place? He had to know by now Brod outstripped him as a polo player. Then there was the tantalising presence of the beautiful, unusual Rebecca. What middle-aged man, however wealthy, would set out to woo a young woman then expose her to the likes of Brod for goodness' sake.

It didn't make a scrap of sense unless Stewart was applying yet another test.

Stewart was a great one for putting people through hoops. Such an arrogant man. Perhaps if the seemingly perfect Rebecca didn't pass the test she would fall from her golden pedestal and be made so uncomfortable she would be forced to leave. Fee was now certain her brother had marriage on his mind and it wasn't out of the question. Even after all these years. Not that they had been womanless. Stewart had had his affairs from time to time but he had obviously never found the woman he wanted to keep for himself. The prize possession. Lucille lovely as a summer's day had been that for a time but somehow Lucille had found the courage to run away. The next one wouldn't be given the opportunity.

Fee didn't like to think it could be Rebecca. She was worried Rebecca might be someone who'd been hurt so badly she could settle for security. An older man, rich, social, establishment, grounded in the conventions. Rebecca could easily mistake an impressive facade for safety.

CHAPTER THREE

HOURS later, in the golden heat of mid-afternoon, Rebecca found herself watching the main polo match of the day with her heart in her throat. She'd enjoyed the morning matches played with such high spirits and comradeship but this was another league again.

All the players were exceptionally fast and focused, the ponies superbly trained especially with all those clubs swinging near their heads and the competition it seemed to her anxious, dazzled eyes exceptionally fierce.

Once she thought Stewart charging at full tilt would come off his horse trying to prevent his son driving the ball through the goal posts. He didn't succeed but it appeared to Rebecca to be too dangerous an effort. For all his fitness and splendid physique, Stewart was in his mid-fifties. No match really for the turning, twisting, speeding Broderick, the most dashing player on the field, though the commanding Cameron brothers ran him close. But for sheer daring, Brod Kinross had the added edge if only to beat his father. They certainly acted as if they were engaged in a highly stylised joust.

"That was close," Rebecca, a little frightened, murmured to Fee who was lounging in a deck chair beside her. "I thought Stewart would be flung out of the saddle."

Trying to impress you, my dear, Fee thought. "It's a dangerous game, darling. I had a dear friend, Tommy Fairchild, killed on the polo field. That was some years ago in England but I think of him almost every other

31

day. Brod's a dare devil. I think it's important to him to even up a few scores."

"Meaning?" Rebecca turned her head to stare into Fee's eyes, finding them covered by very expensive sunglasses.

"Good Lord, Rebecca, I know how perceptive you are," Fee said. "Didn't it strike you that afternoon you met Stewart and Brod that they don't get on."

"Perhaps a little." She kept the fact she'd overheard them quarrelling to herself.

"Darling, you can't fool me. You've noticed, all right. Both of them were trying but it's just something they have to live with."

"But you said Brod has to even up the score?" Just to speak his name gave her a peculiar thrill.

"Brod has been on the receiving end for a long time," Fee confided. "I dote on him as you know. And Alison. I'm going to make sure you meet her. Stewart became very withdrawn after the children's mother left. Brod, despite the fact he's a Kinross through and through, has his mother's beautiful eyes. Perhaps looking into them brings up too many painful memories for Stewart." After all it wasn't inconceivable.

"Do you really think that?" Even Rebecca sounded sceptical.

"No." Fee delicately grimaced. "The truth is Stewart wasn't cut out to be a father. Not every man is."

"Then Brod and his sister must have suffered?" Rebecca rested back in the recliner prepared to listen.

"Assuredly, my dear," Fee agreed. "Money can't bring everything to life, not that I've ever been without it," she had the grace to admit. "But so far as Brod is concerned his upbringing has only made him tougher.

Unlike his little mother. Petite, like you. Lucille was her name. Pretty as a picture.'' Fee's mind instantly conjured up a vision of Lucille on her wedding day. Young, radiant, madly in love with her Stewart. She'd flown home to be Lucille's chief bridesmaid. Her little pal from their schooldays but she'd never been around to lend Lucille her support. She'd been too busy becoming a celebrity.

"She didn't last long," Rebecca observed sadly, echoing Fee's own thoughts.

"No. It was all quite dreadful. You can't imagine how shocked I was when I got the news. Sir Andy rang me. I always called my father that. He was knighted by the Queen for his services to the pastoral industry.''

Something Rebecca already knew. "Stewart didn't ring you?'' she interrupted gently.

"No,'' Fee answered rather grimly, then remained silent for a time.

Sensitive to her pain Rebecca changed the subject. "I have to say I'll be relieved when the match ends,'' she confessed with a wry laugh—Brod's team had scored another goal. "I can't really enjoy it with my heart in my throat.''

"You're a tender little thing.'' Fee moved to pat her hand. "Though at this level I agree it's pretty lethal and Stewart and Brod are going at it hammer and tongs. Half-time coming up. Ten minutes usually. Stewart is bound to want to know if you're enjoying yourself. If I were you, my dear, I'd tell him you're finding it all terribly exciting.''

"But I am.'' Rebecca twisted to smile at Fee, marvelling as ever at her glamorous appearance. "I just don't want anyone to get hurt.''

"Ah, look at Brod,'' Fee broke in gleefully. "Isn't

he luv-er-ly," she cried, Eliza Doolittle style. He was
indeed. On the other side of the field Broderick Kinross
was stripping off his polo shirt to exchange it for another. His jet-black hair, thick and waving, gleamed in
the sunlight with a matt of dark hair spreading across
his darkly tanned chest then narrowing down to his
close fitting jodhpurs.

He was an incredibly handsome man. So much so
Rebecca felt a sudden uprush of desire that alarmed her.
Not that he was flaunting his splendid body or paying
any attention to the heated glances of the female spec-
tators enjoying the spectacle from around the field. He
was too busy sharing a joke with his friend, Rafe
Cameron.

Rebecca wished for a moment she had a camera.
She'd like to photograph these two magnificent young
men together. Of a height, wonderfully fit, perfect foils.
Brod for all his brilliant blue eyes was dark, deeply
tanned by the sun whereas his friend had a thick mane
of pure gold hair that was quite stunning. The other
brother, Grant, busy chatting up a pretty girl, shared the
family fairness, but his hair was more tawny with a
touch of red. Both she had remarked when introduced
had hazel-gold flecked eyes.

"Quite something aren't they?" Fee hooted, following Rebecca's gaze. "A pride of lions only Brod is the
panther among them."

"They're all very handsome," Rebecca agreed. "I'm
surprised they're not all married."

Fee shook her beautifully coiffured head. As dark as
Rebecca's until her fifties she was now close to blond.
"But surely you know?"

"Know what?" Rebecca stared directly at her. More
revelations?

"I thought Stewart might have mentioned it," Fee said. He certainly spent enough time chatting to Rebecca. "At one time we all hoped Rafe and Alison would tie the knot. They were very much in love but somehow Alison got cold feet. Product of a broken home perhaps. She ran off to Sydney much as I ran off to London, though I left no great love behind.

"As we know she's become highly successful. So life goes on. Wild horses wouldn't get it out of him but I believe Rafe was devastated. At any rate he won't allow Alison back into his life.

"As for Brod. He's a hot favourite. Always has been. But Brod will make darn sure he picks the right woman. Grant is a couple of years younger than both of them. He's been working terribly hard establishing his helicopter business. All three are big catches for the girls."

"I'll bet!" Rebecca smiled. "Stewart did tell me a little about Alison's broken romance."

"So are you interested?" Fee pulled herself up to capture Rebecca's luminous gaze.

"My career is important to me, Fee," Rebecca answered lightly.

"A woman can't do without love in her life."

"So I'm learning from your biography," Rebecca quipped instantly.

"Cheeky." Fee smacked at Rebecca's slender arm playfully. "Don't leave it too late, darling. That's all." She spread a beringed hand. "Here comes Stewart. He doesn't look quite as enthusiastic as he did at the start of the match."

"Brod didn't exactly give him any quarter," Rebecca pointed out dryly.

"Each man for himself on the polo field, my chick," Fee drawled in her distinctive voice, which still had so much sex appeal in it. "How's it going, Stewie?" she called a little tauntingly, entirely on her nephew's side.

Stewart Kinross studied his sister rather stonily for a moment then said with slight indignance. "We're doing fairly well. Anything can happen in the second half." He switched his glance to Rebecca, dressed like Fee in a silk shirt and narrow cut linen pants only her outfit was pristine white whereas Fee was a kaleidoscope of colours and patterns with a lot of glitter he didn't find attractive. "You're loving it aren't you, Rebecca." He smiled at her, a remarkably handsome, mature man.

"I'm a little worried for you, Stewart," Rebecca admitted truthfully. "It's a dangerous game."

As a response it was a disaster. "I like to think I keep up, my dear," he answered, looking a bit huffed.

"Oh, Stewart, you do know what I mean," Rebecca protested softly.

He looked deep into her eyes seeing God knows what. "That's fine then, my dear. It's Brod who's putting himself at risk. Maybe you could tell him to his face." He looked back towards the field. "Though I must have done something right...I taught him all he knows. Sometimes I wish I hadn't. Ah well." He glanced back to smile at Rebecca. "I must be off. Time's up."

Rebecca realised she shouldn't say, "Take care." Instead she gave a little encouraging wave while Fee, enjoying every moment, bit back a laugh. "Darling, were you really suggesting Stewie is over the hill?"

A soft little cushion was to hand. Rebecca used it.

"Hey, hey." Fee leaned forward and caught it. "Stewie doesn't like to think he's settling into the twilight zone. For that matter neither do I."

In the end Brod's team won and Rebecca watched as

a tall, good-looking blonde in skin-tight jeans and a blue T-shirt that showed off her shapely breasts, went up to him, threw her arms around his neck and kissed him with much relish.

"Liz Carrol," Fee said with a grin. "She likes him. Can't you tell? Then again, why hide it?"

"Is she his girlfriend?" Rebecca found herself asking, though she hadn't intended to.

"What do you think? Brod sees a few others but most of the time he's just too darned busy. He's got a big job—for life. When he picks a wife he'd better pick well."

Eventually it was Rebecca's turn to congratulate the winning team, standing before the captain wondering why she felt so terribly perturbed by a pair of brilliant blue eyes. Had anyone ever looked at her like that? What kind of look was it? Whatever it was it acted like a magnet.

"Fee told me you were a little anxious at the action," he said leaning back against a rail, looking down at her. Oh, yes, she was beautiful.

Rebecca nodded unapologetically. "Today was my first experience of polo. I have to admit some of it scared me. I thought Stewart would be thrown from his horse at one stage during the first half."

"You were concerned."

She stared up at him, revealing nothing. "Why not?"

He shrugged and flung an arm up to rest on the rail. "He's been thrown before and survived. We all have. I'm curious to know, what do you think of my father?"

"I'm sure I'm not supposed to say I hate him," she said coolly. "I think he's many things. As are you."

"Include yourself in that, Miss Hunt," he answered sardonically, studying the way her dark satiny hair curved around her face. What did she do? Polish it with a silk scarf? "Even Fee knows remarkably little about you."

"Have you asked?" she challenged, her rain coloured eyes widening.

"Indeed I have."

"I can't imagine why you'd be interested in me." Yet she bit her lovely full lower lip. "I'm sure you have many a dramatic revelation to divulge," he drawled. "I'm just blunt enough to point out you're turning my father's head. It's not often I see him take such glowing pleasure in a young woman's company."

"I think you're exaggerating." Perhaps she, too, would have made an actress.

He laughed. "Then why is that magnolia skin stained with colour?"

"It could be your lack of discretion," she countered.

"Actually I'm trying to be frank. You've only been on Kimbara a short time yet you've made a considerable impact on my father and Fee."

"Obviously not *you*." She was still managing to speak with perfect calm even if she couldn't control the fire in her blood.

A taut smile crossed his striking face. "I'm not as susceptible as Dad or as trusting as Fee."

"Goodness you ought to set yourself up in the detective business." She kept her voice low in case anyone was watching. They were.

"Come on, all I'm suggesting is you tell me a little more about yourself."

"You won't find my face in a rogue's gallery if that's what you're thinking." She stared back at him.

"How about an art gallery?" he suggested. "Your

style of looks is incredibly romantic. In fact they ought to name a flower after you."

"No artist has offered to paint me so far," she told him. "What exactly is it you suspect me of, Mr. Kinross?"

Her face was still flushed, her eyes as lustrous as silver. "You're angry with me and quite rightly." He dropped his hand off the rail and stood straight. Another foot and their bodies would be brushing.

"*I* think so."

"But from where I'm standing I think you might be trying to steal my father's heart."

She felt so affronted she tossed her silky mane in the air. "Part of it might be because *you're* screwed up."

He stared back at her for a moment then threw back his handsome head and gave a genuine peal of laughter. A warm seductive sound. "I'm not hearing this," he groaned. "You think *I'm* screwed up."

"It must be a very heavy load to carry," she said without sympathy.

He laughed again, white teeth dazzling against dark copper skin. "Actually you might be right."

"We've all got our hang-ups to disengage," she pointed out with clinical cool.

"I can hardly wait to hears yours."

"You're not going to hear them, Mr. Kinross."

"*Pleez,*" he mocked. "If we're going to have these conversations you'd better call me Brod."

It was a mystery to her she was keeping her cool. "Thank you for that. I'd love it if you called me Rebecca. All I'm asking, *Brod,* is you give me the benefit of the doubt before starting to label me 'adventuress.' From what I've seen, your father is perfectly charming to women in general."

"Isn't that the truth," he answered, his voice dangerously gentle. "Charming, yes. Possessive, no."

"Is that how you read it?" She kept the worry out of her tone.

"Most women can't resist being the object of desire."

She felt as if they were engaged in some ritual dance, circling, circling. "That's something I know nothing about." She'd been determined to play it cool but her simmering temper was making her eyes sparkle.

"Quite impossible, Rebecca." His lips curved. "If you put on your dowdiest dress and cut off that waterfall of hair, men would still want you."

She had the disturbing sensation he had reached out and touched her, run his fingers over her skin. "I don't think you've reckoned on whether I want them," she answered, too sharply, as her heart did a double take.

His blue eyes filled with amused mockery. "Now where is this leading us?"

"Probably nowhere." She managed a shrug. "The whole conversation was your idea."

"Only because I'm trying to learn as much about you as I can." He realised he was getting an undeniable charge out of what amounted to their confrontation. It was like being exposed to live wires.

"I'm thoroughly aware of that," Rebecca said, "but I do hope you're not going to start checking on me. I might have to mention it to your father."

Ah, an admission of power. Why had he ever had one minute's doubt? His eyes narrowed, lean body tensing. "I'll be damned, a threat."

She shook her head. "No threat at all. I'm not going to allow you to spoil things for me, that's all."

"I can do that by checking you out?"

"That's not what I meant at all." Her voice went very quiet. "I'm here in one capacity only. To write your aunt's biography. Both of us want it done. It's a pity you've made up your mind I've more on the agenda. It's almost like you're waging war."

"Isn't it," he agreed.

"Perhaps you've got nothing to win." She threw out the challenge, suddenly wanting to hurt him as he was hurting her.

"Well we can't say the same for you then."

The sapphire eyes gleamed.

Both of them were so involved in the cut and thrust, neither noticed Stewart Kinross approach until he was only a few yards away. "I was trying to make out what you two were talking about?" He smiled, though it never quite reached his eyes.

"Why don't I let Rebecca tell you," Brod drawled.

"Clearly it was something serious," his father said. "Everybody else seems to be laughing and relaxed."

"Brod was taking me through the technicalities of the match." Rebecca was worried her voice might tremble but it didn't. It sounded very normal. "I'm hoping to understand the game better."

"But, my dear, I could have explained all that," Stewart Kinross assured her warmly. "Sure it wasn't something more interesting?"

Rebecca twisted round to look at Brod. "Nothing except a few words about my work."

"I'm sure it will be so good you'll have people dying to read it," Brod said suavely. "Ah well, I'd better circulate. Some of my friends I haven't seen for a long time."

This caused Stewart to frown. "You can see them anytime you want to, Brod."

"I guess I'm too damned busy, Dad. Especially since you promoted me. See you later, Rebecca." He lifted a hand, moving off before his father could say another word.

Stewart Kinross's skin reddened. "I must apologise for my son, Rebecca," he rasped.

"Whatever for?" She was anxious not to become involved.

"His manner," Stewart replied. "It worries me sometimes. I've had to deal with a lot of rivalry from Brod."

"I suppose it's not that unusual," Rebecca tried to soothe. "powerful father, powerful son. It must make for clashes from time to time."

"None of them, I assure you, initiated by me," Stewart protested. "Brod takes after my father. He was combative by nature."

"And generally regarded as a great man?" Rebecca murmured gently just to let him know she had read up extensively on Sir Andrew Kinross and liked what she had learned.

"Yes, there's that," Stewart agreed a little grudgingly. "He positively doted on Fee. Denied her nothing that's why she's so terribly spoiled. But he expected a great deal of me. Anyway, enough of that. What I really wanted to know is did you enjoy the day? I organised the whole thing for you."

"I realise that, Stewart. It's something I'll always remember." Rebecca tasted a certain bitterness on her tongue. Remember? But for wrong reasons. Most of the time her eyes had been glued to Broderick Kinross's dashing figure. She could still feel the rush of adrenaline through her body.

"You know, sometimes I get the feeling I've known

you forever," Stewart Kinross announced, resting a hand on her shoulder and staring down into her eyes. "Don't you get that feeling, too?"

What on earth do I say? Rebecca thought, suffused with embarrassment. Whatever I say he seems to misinterpret it. She allowed her long thick lashes to feather down onto her cheeks. "Maybe we're kindred spirits, Stewart," she said. "Fee says the same thing."

It was far from being the response Stewart Kinross wanted, but he knew damned well he would never give up. Many good years remained of his life. Maybe Rebecca was a little young. It didn't strike him as *too* young. In their conversations she sounded remarkably mature, in control. Besides, as his wife she would be well compensated. He was definitely a very rich man and if that had to do increasingly more with Brod's managerial skills he wasn't about to admit it.

Meanwhile half-way across the field Brod, the centre of an admiring circle, continued to observe this disturbing tableau. They could have been father and daughter, he thought with the cold wings of anger. Only he could read his father's body language from a mile. Her dark head so thick and glossy reached just about to his father's heart as it would his. Her face was uptilted. She looked very slender and delicate in her outfit, boyish except for the swell of her breasts. His father's hand had come up to rest on one of her fine-boned shoulders. He was staring down into her eyes. God, the utter impossibility of it but it was happening. His father had fallen in love. The thought shocked him profoundly. He turned away abruptly, grateful that his friend, Rafe, was approaching with a cold can of beer. A black fairy story this.

* * *

Rebecca stood before the mirror holding two dresses in front of her in turn. One was lotus-pink, the other a beaded silk chiffon in a dusky green. Both were expensive, hanging from shoe-string straps and coming just past the knee rather like the tea dresses of the early 1930s when women looked like hot-house blooms. It was the sort of look she liked and one that suited her petite figure. Fee had told her much earlier their guests liked to dress up so now she studied her reflection trying to decide which dress looked best. She was glad she'd packed them, though again Fee had advised her at the outset to bring a couple of pretty evening dresses.

"Stewart likes to entertain whenever the opportunity presents itself."

Hence the polo weekend. And all for her. Only a couple of weeks ago it would have given her the greatest pleasure. Now the fact that Stewart Kinross had somehow become infatuated with her raised a lot of anxieties. Not the least of them Broderick Kinross's attitude.

Knowing his father better than anyone else he had immediately divined the exact quality of Stewart's interest. She would bet every penny she had Brod believed she had gone along with the situation. Even encouraged it.

Becoming involved with a much older man was one thing. Becoming involved with a *very rich* older man was another. It happened all the time and society accepted powerful influential men could get anything they wanted. Lots of money, it seemed, made a deep impression on everyone.

Stewart Kinross, if he suddenly remarried, could even father another family, increasing the number of heirs to the family fortune. It all left Rebecca feeling freezing cold. Life had been terrible when she had had a man in her life. She'd been so young and she had had no idea what jealousy and obsession meant. But she had learned. How she had learned!

Rebecca stared at her haunted eyes in the mirror. She was standing absolutely still, holding the lovely dusky green dress in front of her like a shield. She told herself she didn't care what Broderick Kinross thought. His suspicions understandable maybe were absolutely groundless. From her first day at Kimbara she had considered Stewart Kinross to be an exceptionally charming and generous man. Now she saw that might not be the case. The only thing that was becoming increasingly clear was he was smitten. She had seen that look of possession in a man's eyes before. She didn't want to see it again.

Abruptly Rebecca turned away from the mirror. The green dress would do. It even lent some of its colour to her eyes. She wasn't afraid of Broderick Kinross, either, though she half dreaded seeing him tonight. If she really were an adventuress looking to snaffle his rich father she couldn't have made more of an enemy. In a way she understood. A new wife would automatically become part heiress to the Kinross fortune. Perhaps gain a controlling interest. She was probably right at this moment news. A few of the women guests hadn't been able to hide their speculation. Thank God Fee was on her side. She had come out here simply to write a celebrity's biography, never thinking she could be catapulted into a Situation.

Almost an hour later, when Rebecca was ready to go downstairs and mingle with the guests, a knock came at her door. She went to it expecting to see Fee resplendent in one of her stunning outfits only Stewart

Kinross stood outside the door holding a long velvet box in his hand.

Rebecca moved forward a little blindly not wanting to invite him into the bedroom.

"My dear girl, you look absolutely beautiful," he said, his strongly boned face softening into undisguised admiration. "I love your dress. It's perfect."

"And you look very distinguished, Stewart," she said, edging a little along the painting hung in the hallway. Indeed he did. Commanding, fastidious with the physical presence of someone much younger. Only the eyes were a shade predatory, she thought out of sheer nervousness. What on earth was in that navy velvet box? Not a present surely. She was far from enraptured. She was dismayed.

"Perhaps we could go back into your room for a moment," he said in his now familiar richly modulated tones. "More private with guests in the house. I couldn't be more pleased with your choice of dress, the colour, the style. I have something here I thought you might like to wear tonight. A family heirloom I must of course take back but I notice you didn't bring much jewellery with you...probably not expecting a do like this."

She hadn't the slightest intention of accepting. "Stewart, I really feel..." she began, watching him raise a heavy black eyebrow.

"You can't refuse a simple request, my dear. I want to show you off."

"Whatever for, Stewart?" She tried the wide-eyed look. "They must know I'm only here to write Fee's biography."

"I wonder if you realise you've found your way into

our hearts, Rebecca. I'm sure you'll be gracious, my dear. Especially when you see this."

Somehow he had compelled her to move backwards into the lovely cream-and-gold room with its antique French bedroom suite, its fine paintings and porcelain objects. She'd never been in such a bedroom in all her life.

A few feet into the room she turned to face her host. He was wearing a white dinner jacket and a white shirt with his black evening trousers, black tie, his thick dark hair deeply waving like his son's winged with silver. "This hasn't seen the light of day for some time," he said, lifting an exquisite necklace from its container before turning to set the container down on a cabinet.

"Stewart, that looks very important." She just managed to keep her voice from wavering. Appended from a gold chain was a truly magnificent large oval opal flashing a beautiful play of colours, the legendary gem stone surrounded by full cut glittering diamonds.

"Important to our family, yes." He smiled, his large tanned hands undoing the delicate catch. "There's quite a story attached to this opal," he said. "When I have the time I'll tell you but our guests will be waiting."

She tried once more to refuse, knowing the sort of man he was, knowing she might offend him. "Stewart, if you don't mind, I can't wear such an obviously valuable thing. Besides in some quarters opals are said to be unlucky."

"Rubbish!" He banished that idea with a snort. "The Greeks and the Romans valued opals very highly as well they might. Queen Victoria loved the opals that were sent to her from her Australian colonies. The royal jewellers made her up many magnificent pieces. A big opal strike made the Kinross and Cameron fortunes. So no more talk of that, my dear. This will complement the lovely green of your dress. It's almost as though you knew what I had in mind. Be a good girl now," he said cajolingly, "Hold up your hair."

Short of an argument Rebecca thought she had little option. She held her long hair away from her neck while Stewart placed the necklace around it and did up the catch.

"There, what did I tell you?" He took infinite pleasure in her appearance. She was sheer perfection from her gleaming head to her pretty narrow feet in evening shoes whose colour exactly matched her silvery beaded dress.

She thought she'd find herself bright pink with embarrassment when she turned around swiftly to face the long pier mirror. She of all people knew how dangerous it was to court obsession. How much it could devastate a life.

But the necklace was beautiful. So beautiful lying against her bare skin.

"My God you're lovely," she heard Stewart say, his voice surprisingly harsh. "Lovely in just the way I like."

Why hadn't she seen what this could lead to? Was she a fool? Did she think she was protected by the big age difference?

"I think after all I'll take it off, Stewart," she said quite strongly.

"No." He sensed immediately he was giving too much away. He urged caution on himself. He always took getting what he wanted for granted but this young woman was different—very special.

"Rebecca, Stewart?" Fee, looking every inch the star of the theatre surprised them by appearing in the open doorway, her shrewd glance going from one to the other. "What's the problem?"

"Good God, what are you talking about. There's no problem, Fee," her brother responded testily. "You seem to be wearing a billion dollars around your neck. I thought Rebecca might like the loan of a necklace."

Now Rebecca turned full into the light looking back at Fee, her beautiful eyes so lambent they might have been fighting back tears. Fee made an instinctive clutch at the doorjamb, feeling shocked, appalled and astounded all at once. She had been waiting for something to happen, she'd been getting little intimations right through Rebecca's stay—now it was literally before her.

Rebecca was wearing Cecilia's Necklace against her creamy breast. The last time Fee had seen it, Lucille had been wearing it. As was her right. Cecilia's Necklace had been handed down through the generations to each successive mistress of Kimbara. Fee remembered it on her own mother when Fee was a girl. It took her some moments to straighten, superb actress though she was, her inner disturbance detectable in her marvellous green eyes.

"Don't you think I'm right, Fee?" Stewart knowing her reaction, tried to circumvent a rash answer.

What do I do? Fee thought, looking back at her brother. Make a scene? In that instant she knew she couldn't, scenting danger. Kimbara and everything on it was Stewart's while he lived and he was given to considerable hauteur. Rebecca's slender figure seemed to be quivering. It was obvious she, too, was shocked by Stewart's gesture even without knowing anything of the opal's history. Unless Stewart had told her?

"I haven't seen that in a long time," Fee managed to remark with her nephew's trademark irony.

"It deserves an airing." Stewart was uncomfortably aware Rebecca's face was looking flushed, when he knew he had to treat her like a piece of priceless china.

"It looks absolutely wonderful on you, Rebecca," Fee said enmeshed in a dilemma. Weren't men fools? "And it goes beautifully with your dress." Rebecca would writhe in shame if she advised her to take it off and she was much too fond of the younger woman to do that. From the beginning they had fallen into a warm, easy camaraderie.

"I was concerned it was too valuable," Rebecca said, grateful beyond belief for Fee's comforting presence. The sheer awfulness of it! She just knew in her bones wearing the necklace wasn't right.

"You're amongst family and friends, my dear," Stewart assured her with a sudden shift to the avuncular. "There's no question of its becoming lost or stolen."

No, but it was going to cause a great many surprises, Fee thought wretchedly. For Brod above all...

Downstairs in the homestead's huge drawing room with its striped silk walls and splendid curtains at the sets of French doors, the oriental and European furnishings, the guests were assembled enjoying drinks before they all wandered over to the Great Hall where there would be dancing and a sumptuous buffet. The band had been flown in along with a well-known TV personality to act as compere, and the caterers had spent most of the weekend labouring to make everything a great success. Stewart Kinross always paid well but he expected everything to be first-rate and was furious when it wasn't. The owner of one catering firm had once hinted, "Ugly".

Living in isolation for so much of the time Outback people revelled in these occasions and as Rebecca accompanied Stewart and Fee down the sweeping staircase she could hear the steady hum of conversation and banter, the sound of music and laughter. Partying was what it was all about. She was acutely aware she was being treated like family of some sort. Certainly not the journalist who had been hired to write Fiona Kinross's biography.

As they reached the parquet floor of the Front Hall, which was what the family called the spacious entrance, several guests flowed out to meet them, Broderick Kinross among them such a blaze in his eyes Rebecca felt herself vibrating like a plucked string. She had the impression something about her had transfixed him. He was certainly staring at her, his gaze so sizzling she felt she might melt like wax. Maybe he objected violently to her wearing a valuable family necklace.

Other people on the verge of calling out appeared to fall silent, a gap Fee instantly filled with great self-assurance.

"Now, my darlings, what say we all have another glass of champagne, then it will be time to adjourn to the Great Hall. We can't have the band sitting around entertaining themselves now, can we?"

The blonde, Liz Carrol, in a slinky Armani red jersey, said something into Broderick Kinross's ear, something that deepened the fire in his eyes. Something Rebecca was convinced was about *her*.

They all went back into the drawing room, Rebecca accepting her first glass of champagne of the night, though some of the guests appeared to have had a good many already. One of the young men who had played on Stewart's team, Stephen Mellor, turned to her smiling, telling her how lovely she looked. He'd heard it from Brod the young woman who was writing Fee's biography was as "stylised as an orchid" something indefinable about Brod indicating she didn't appeal, but Rebecca Hunt was really something. He started to ask her to save some dances for him when Rebecca caught Broderick Kinross's eyes across the room. He gave her a salute with his crystal flute of such mockery Rebecca felt it bordered more on contempt, then turned back to his companion, Liz Carrol.

"I think we might all walk across now," Stewart announced after about ten minutes, taking Rebecca's arm in a courtly sort of way. "You're going to love what they've done to the Hall, Rebecca. This new firm I got in knows how to rise to the occasion."

The black velvet sky was ablaze with stars, the breeze that blew in from the desert surprisingly cool.

Leaving Liz with their friends, Brod caught up with his aunt, drawing her a little to one side. "Damn it, Fee, what's Dad up to?" he asked in a deep growl.

"I've never known him to act like this," Fee confessed. "Not since the early days when he was courting your mother."

"And the necklace! What in hell are we supposed to make of her wearing it?"

Fee lifted a graceful hand and hunched her shoulders. "Darling, I'm as frantic as you are. I had absolutely no idea this was going to happen." Which at least was the truth.

"But why? And why tonight?" Brod groaned. "You can bet your life everyone will be talking about it. It sure made Rafe and Grant sit up and take notice."

"I'll bet!" Fee agreed wryly. "Darling, we can't talk about this now." The breeze made the long skirt of her black chiffon gown swirl around her and she held it down. "We have guests. All of them with big ears."

"They're not taking any notice of us," Brod pointed out crisply. "Most of them have gone ahead. Dad must have told her the story?"

"I really don't know." Fee shook her head worriedly. "I'm absolutely sure Rebecca wasn't expecting it. I suspect Stewart is entirely responsible for her wearing it."

Brod reacted explosively. "God she looks like Rose White in the fairy tale and she's a miserable little gold-digger."

Fee had never known him so coldly angry. "Darling, you're wrong, so wrong. Rebecca is a fine young woman. I think I'm a good judge of character."

"How can I be wrong, Fee," he said, shaking his head, "when it's as clear as crystal. I remember vividly my mother wearing that opal with her beautiful hair drawn back. This isn't a break with tradition. I'm starting to believe Dad intends to marry your Miss Hunt."

Fee gave a deep sigh. "I'm afraid he might be thinking along those lines, but he'll have a job trying to convince Rebecca to marry him."

"What do you really know about this girl?" Brod retaliated. "Some women love money. Maybe she didn't come here with anything in mind, then again maybe she did?" Along with his feelings of outrage Brod felt almost as though he'd been doubly betrayed.

"That isn't quite how it happened," Fee decided to confide. "Your father set it all up."

"Wha-t?" He sounded stunned.

"Stewart saw Rebecca on television when she was being interviewed about Judith's book. He liked what he saw and persuaded me to approach her."

"Dad did?" Brod started to move like a restive thoroughbred.

"Darling, at that time a biography hadn't entered my head." Fee put a soothing hand on his white jacketed arm. "I was home for a visit, half pleasure, half business. Your father was trying to talk me into selling a lot of my company shares. He has the right to buy me out as you know."

"Don't do it, Fee," Brod warned. "There are all sorts of issues involved."

"I told you I wouldn't." She shook her head. "Stewart persuaded me I had a story to tell. I fell for it hook, line and sinker, vain creature that I am."

"Dad would do that?" He was amazed.

"He must be lonely, Brod. Rattling round in a mansion all by himself," Fee offered by way of explanation.

"He's had a dozen opportunities to remarry over the years. Roz Bennet was a nice woman."

"Indeed she was. And is. But she doesn't fill the role of object of desire. Stewart doesn't find it easy to love, Brod. We all know that. You and Ally especially."

"This is infatuation, Fee," Brod told her grimly. "Obsession if you like and you know what they say, obsession blurs the vision. This girl is only a bit older than Ally. In other words she's young enough to be his daughter."

"It happens, Brod," Fee said in deep wry tones.

He shook his head, scrapped his chiselled chin. "I have to tell you I'm shocked."

"I'm finding it a bit unseemly myself and I've seen everything," Fee agreed dryly.

"Miss Hunt must really fancy herself as a femme fatale."

"Darling, is it bothering you a great deal?" Fee said

gently, putting a hand on him arm and urging him to walk on towards the brilliant lights of the Great Hall.

"Believe me, it sure as hell is."

It seemed to Rebecca she and Broderick Kinross spent most of the night trading loaded glances but so far he hadn't come near her. What was there to talk about anyway? It couldn't be more obvious he didn't like or approve of her but she received an inordinate amount of attention from his father who repeatedly asked her to sit out dances with him.

"I never did like dancing," Stewart said.

"Really, you manage very well." Rebecca smiled, keeping her tone light.

He looked pleased. "Thank you, my dear, but I'd much prefer it if you could just sit here with me and talk. Well hello there, Michael." He looked up pointedly as a sandy-haired very attractive young man who could never quite get to dance with Rebecca, suddenly marched right up to them.

"Good evening, sir." Michael gave a little bow. "Marvellous party." His snapping brown eyes settled on Rebecca. "How about it, Rebecca? I'd love it if you'd dance with me." He smiled into her eyes.

"Rebecca is a little tired…she's been so much in demand." Stewart Kinross went to shake his leonine head but Rebecca returned the young man's smile warmly and stood up.

"Not at all, Stewart," she said lightly, "I seem to have been sitting most of the night."

Oh well hell, she thought as she moved off. Stewart deserved that.

Thrilled, Michael, nicknamed Sandy for obvious reasons, manoeuvred her onto the floor. "Arrogant old devil isn't he?" he chuckled.

"He isn't old," Rebecca said. "He's a very handsome man."

"Heck the lot of them are," Sandy snorted. "Fee's still a knockout. Ally's a dream. Brod of course is Brod. A knock 'em dead kind of guy. I think Liz has got her pretty little talons into him."

"They're an item are they?" Rebecca wasn't sure she liked that.

"Could be, but Brod's not an easy man to read. Then again we hardly see anything of him nowadays. He's got big responsibilities. They keep him busy. One of these days his dad is going to push him too far."

"Meaning?" Rebecca glanced up quickly.

Michael backed off. "I don't want to explain, Rebecca. I want to have fun. But take my word for it. And what the heck are you doing with that gorgeous chunk of opal around your neck?" He looked down at the glowing opal within its glittery setting.

"Why do you ask?" Rebecca said, she hoped pleasantly.

"Miss Rebecca, it's been causing an incredible amount of interest," Sandy drawled.

"Did it cost a million dollars? Actually I didn't want to wear it," she confided, "but Stewart insisted. I didn't bring much in the way of jewellery with me and he was being kind. I thought it was a family piece not the Crown jewels."

Sandy raised an eyebrow. "Ma'am, in this part of the world it darn near is. You know its story?"

She felt a chill pass through her. "No, I'm afraid not."

For a moment he looked surprised. "It's not as though I'm initiating you into a big secret."

"I love secrets," Rebecca said when in actual fact dismay was creeping over her.

"Then we can't disappoint you," a familiar voice said from just behind her shoulder.

"Ah hell, Brod, you're not going to steal Rebecca away?" Sandy asked with a mixture of disgust and resignation in his voice.

"I really have to speak to her, Sandy. You'll get your turn."

Sandy stared into Rebecca's eyes. "Promise?"

"I promise, Michael," she said, feeling herself tense all over at the thought of being in Broderick Kinross's arms.

"Gosh, I didn't know my name sounded so good," Sandy relinquished her to Brod and moved off, catching another girl around the waist without missing a beat.

"You've created a sensation tonight." Brod was shocked by how natural it seemed to hold her. So natural he had the mad notion to abruptly pull back.

"So it appears," she answered dryly. She tilted her head to look up at him, letting her gaze linger on him. Knowing she was a fool. The sapphire eyes were flashing danger signals, his handsome face taut within its Byronic frame of dark hair. She couldn't imagine a man looking more stunning. Or more elegant for that matter. He showed his breeding. Even in his everyday denim work clothes.

"That's a beautiful dress." He traced a searing glance down her face, her throat, to the lilac shadowed cleft of her breast.

"Thank you." She tossed it off very coolly, though she had trouble catching her breath.

"One needs a beautiful dress if you're going to wear important jewellery."

"You're dancing with me for a reason." She threw down the challenge.

"I think we understand each other." He nodded.

"So it's the necklace?"

"You betcha." He moved her closer as another couple threatened to bump into them.

"So do you want to tell me all about it?" she invited.

"You mean Dad didn't?" He gave her a twisted smile, scepticism pricking his eyes.

"He told me he'd tell me about its history some time." She tried to hide her fluster.

Her ethereal appearance was deceptive, he thought. She really handled herself well under fire. "Its not as though it's a closely guarded secret."

"You'd be doing me a big favour if you'd get on with it," she flared, very slightly.

He stared back at her through appraising eyes. "The necklace you're wearing has been presented to every Kinross bride for generations. *No one* else wears it. Not Fee. Not my sister. I last saw it adorning my mother's neck. You'll know already the Kinross Cameron fortunes were largely built on a big opal strike in 1860?"

"Yes, I've read all about that," she confirmed, shock pouring into her. "Fee has told me a great deal more."

"Yet no one mentioned Cecilia's Necklace?"

His cynicism was intolerable. "That's what I'm wearing?"

"The magnolia image is just right for it. How smart of Dad to realise."

"I didn't want to wear it," she answered him, her voice like cut glass.

"But you have such a sense of style."

"Your father insisted." She tried to swallow a tide of feelings. "I didn't like to offend him."

"Would you have worn whatever dress he wanted as well?"

The music momentarily stopped. All the guests applauded wildly. It was her moment to escape but he kept a light hold of her arm, trapping her like a fluttering bird in a cage.

"I really don't have to put up with this," she said after a stricken minute. Every pulse in her body was jumping.

"You really do." He glanced over her satin sheened dark head at the swirling dancers. "You're free to go back and sit beside Dad as soon as I've done."

"I can walk off right now." Yet his magnetism was a powerful thing.

"Try it," he said very quietly, a warning in his eyes.

"Bullies don't appeal to me." Her mind and her senses were furiously at war.

"I wouldn't dream of bullying you." His touch gentled. "By the same token, devious little Scarlett O'Hara types don't appeal to me."

"You're talking nonsense."

God wasn't he? He felt incredibly mixed up but his voice was hard. "Not after what's happened tonight. Every last person here witnessed it. They'll all go off to spread the news."

"Which is?" Her heart was beating so swiftly she hated him.

"You have considerable standing in my father's eyes. Not to say power."

"Perhaps he was just being kind." She knew he wasn't.

Brod laughed. "Being kind isn't quite Dad's style.

Hell, Miss Hunt, he might as well have given you a great big engagement ring. I know my mother's was a flawless four carat solitaire. It's still in the safe.''

She broke clear of him suddenly but he caught her hand, drawing her off the floor towards a stand of golden canes that had been brought in for decoration.

''I'm genuinely shocked at what you're saying.'' She swung to face him. In fact a kind of fear tore through her.

''Out of what? Guilty you've been sprung?''

''How charming you are.'' She wanted desperately to abandon herself to rage but it wasn't her way.

''I want you to take me very seriously.'' Out of the corner of his eye he could see his father stalking towards them. His father. Almost his enemy.

''Oh, I do.'' She shrank away a little, her beautiful eyes darkening with intensity.

''Obviously you're hugely concerned your father might remarry. It's even possible you might no longer be heir.'' She yielded into giving this taunt.

He stared down at her, discovering he wanted to kiss that mouth. Crush it. ''Sorry to disappoint you,'' he said with sleek humour. ''My inheritance is all tied up. Even Dad can't change it. But keep talking, Rebecca, I want to know your plans.''

''What would be the point,'' she answered with cool scorn, shrugging a delicate shoulder. ''You've made up your mind about me.''

''Well, you've been able to do something Ally and I could never manage,'' he pointed out very dryly. ''You have my father eating out of your hand.'' Brod turned his dark head. ''Ah, here Dad comes. In which case I'll excuse myself. I'm sure he'll take care of you, Miss Hunt.''

*　　*　　*

Rebecca didn't think she could get through the night, though outwardly she acted with considerable panache. It was, she realised, her training. She had to meet fear with calm. She wasn't going to have the opal around her neck, either. She intended to take it off as soon as she decently could. The fact that Stewart had insisted she wear it upset her profoundly and she didn't blame his son for challenging her so keenly. But why hadn't Fee warned her? Though now she came to think if it, Fee had acted oddly when they were in the bedroom. Fee could have said," I don't think it's a good idea for Rebecca to wear it," but on reflection Rebecca knew why. Stewart Kinross was a man of considerable hauteur. There was probably no one with the exception of his rebel son who dared to tell him what to do.

The buffet was as sumptuous as promised, the long tables with their floor-length starched cloths, hydrangea pink and blue, groaning under so much delicious food it was a wonder they didn't snap with the load. Hams, turkey, chicken dishes, big platters of smoked salmon, seafood airlifted from the Gulf of Carpentaria in far North Queensland, prawns, lobsters, whole baked barramundi, an endless variety of salads, rice and pasta dishes. Hired bartenders handled the drinks, two young waiters circling constantly, the high emotion of the band and its lead singer occasionally drowning all other sound. Couples wandered back and forth between dances enjoying everything that was offered.

Rebecca ate little, though. She was too upset. Instead she spent some time speaking to the Cameron brothers who clearly were too gentlemanly to embarrass her by mentioning the Necklace. Flashes were now going off constantly as most of the guests posed for their photographs to be taken.

Across the room Rebecca saw Broderick Kinross the epicentre of a small group with Liz Carrol holding his hand and smiling brilliantly into his face. Fee was having a great time, too, moving freely from one group to the other, leaving them laughing exuberantly with one of her endless flow of anecdotes.

Eventually she found her way over to Rebecca's side while nice Michael went off to fetch Rebecca a sparkling mineral water. No way was Rebecca going to drink too much. Her whole life was control.

"How's it going?" Fee asked with a warm smile.

Rebecca turned her fawnlike neck, and looked Fee straight in the eye.

"Fee, why didn't you tell me this necklace is never worn by anyone except the Kinross wives?" she demanded.

"Oh Lord!" Fee murmured under her breath, dropping abruptly into a beribboned chair, one of a great many scattered about the beautifully decorated hall. "I really thought Stewart might have told you."

"Come off it, Fee." Rebecca glinted at her. "Would I have worn it had I known?"

"No." Fee shook her head sadly. "Not a nice girl like you."

"Why couldn't you have said something. I really hate being made a fool of."

Fee winced. "I deserve this, I know. But I don't think I have to remind you Stewart is absolutely master in his own home. He wouldn't have taken too kindly to my intervention. Besides I blush to admit it I had the teeniest little doubt you might have known. You and Stewart have grown quite close."

"Good grief!" Rebecca could hardly believe it. "The

only feeling I have for Stewart is respect for his position. Goodness, Fee, I'm half his age.''

"I know that, darling, but you forget I've seen a great deal. Plenty of young women respond to money.''

"Not me," Rebecca said flatly.

"All right, all right." Fee reached over to Rebecca's hand placatingly. "But I'm worldly enough to divine you've suffered a rather bad experience in the past. A broken romance. A sensitive young woman like you might then settle for other things. Security. Safety. You do see what I mean?''

"I still can't believe it. I'm not settling for anything, Fee. I'm quite happy the way I am.'' She chose to think so anyway.

"So if Stewart didn't tell you, who did?'' Fee enquired.

"Your nephew, of course.'' Rebecca shot her a shimmering glance. "And he didn't pull any punches. Boy doesn't he love to sit in judgement!''

"You can't blame him, I suppose,'' Fee said loyally. She had barely recovered herself.

"Actually I don't,'' Rebecca said wryly, "but I've never met anyone so...so...downright hateful in my life.''

"He's upset you.'' Fee's heavily mascared green eyes looked remorseful.

"It kills me to admit it, yes. He actually believes I'm after his father.''

"Gracious, darling, is that so unusual? Look around you. Half the women in this room and that includes the young ones would jump at the chance of becoming Stewart's second wife. He's still a very handsome man and he's megarich. You know what they say...''

"Power is the greatest aphrodisiac.''

"Exactly, darling."

"Well it isn't for me. Not for a moment," Rebecca said straightening the gold chain on the opal necklace, the centre of all the fuss. "As soon as the moment presents itself I'll go back to the house and lock it away."

"Good. I'll try and join you," Fee said. "Not that I know the combination to the safe. Perhaps Brod does."

"Leave *him* out of it." Rebecca's eyes flashed like sun on ice and Fee had to laugh.

"You and he have made the sparks fly between you. I've never seen you furious."

"I've no desire to be, Fee," Rebecca countered earnestly. "I've loved being here on Kimbara. I love working with you on our book but I'm not happy with this...situation that seems to have developed."

"Let me talk to Brod," Fee offered, looking anxiously into Rebecca's serious eyes. "The last thing I want is to lose you. We work so well together and having you in the house brings my daughter a little nearer."

"Of course you miss Francesca." Rebecca was getting to know all about Fee's marriage to her English Earl. How she had one child from it, her only child, Lady Francesca de Lyle, a young woman around Rebecca's own age.

"Of course I do," Fee sighed.

"She still lives with her father?"

"Not any more. She has a place of her own in London. She works in public relations. Rupert bought it for her. He was alway a wonderful father but Fran visits Ormond House often. Takes her friends. Working on the biography has brought it all back. It grieves me now to think I was never there for my little girl when she needed me. All through her schooldays. I wanted to be but somehow I let her down. I had a brilliant career but it made a great many demands on me and my time. Really it ended my marriage. No wonder Fran worships her father. He was both mother and father to her.''

"But the three of you are all at peace now, Fee?'' Very gently Rebecca reached out a sympathetic hand.

"Oh, yes, darling.'' Fee blinked her amazingly long eyelashes. "Rupert has long since remarried. Happily, I'm glad to say. Francesca rings me all the time. I wish I could get her to come out to Australia for a visit. I want you two to meet. Stewart is very fond of Fran. He likes cool, gentle women. I never could keep my emotions under control. Passion always drove me.''

"Which is probably why you're such a marvellous actress,'' Rebecca soothed. "I don't want you to bother having to come with me, Fee. I'll slip over to the house by myself.''

"All right, darling.'' Fee stood up, pressing her chiffon skirt against her trim thighs. "You might slip the necklace into one of the desk drawers in Stewart's study. Lock it, take the key. Explain to Stewart knowing its history you were uncomfortable wearing it.''

Uncomfortable doesn't say it, Rebecca thought, glancing up to see Michael returning with her iced mineral water.

CHAPTER FOUR

As REBECCA moved into the Front Hall she glanced at the French clock on the rosewood panelled wall. Twenty minutes after twelve. It had taken her all of that time to break away quietly from the guests. The gala evening was still going on in earnest. Another classic Outback gathering though Rebecca doubted many of them could be so lavish. Stewart had planned it all like a military manoeuvre, his organisation first-class. He had even decided on the flowers. Her mind blanked out *all for her.*

The revelries would go on until breakfast for those who were still standing. She would be really enjoying herself only for the fact Stewart had trapped her into wearing an important family heirloom, thus spoiling everything. What was his reason? To let people know he had his eyes on an attractive young woman he was considering as a potential wife?

It was a great pity he hadn't taken the trouble to ask *her!* He simply accepted he could have any woman he liked.

What arrogance!

The magnificent old homestead was very quiet though lights bloomed in all the major rooms and several of the bedrooms upstairs. Rebecca found her way to Stewart's study with its massive desk and cabinets, its hundreds of books, sporting trophies, marvellous paintings of horses being held by attendants and over the fireplace a large portrait of Stewart's late father,

Brod's grandfather, Sir Andrew Kinross. It was placed exactly so the eyes followed the viewer around the room.

Rebecca paused for a moment to look up at him. Sir Andrew had been a very impressive looking man. Big, handsome, distinguished. Yes, the family face. But the eyes a clear green were so *kind,* Rebecca thought. Kind, calm and wise. Stewart's were filled with power, prestige, control. Those were the things that evidently mattered to him.

Broderick Kinross's brilliant blue eyes...burned with banked fires. She realised he was awakening in her feelings that could spiral out of control unless she clamped down hard. She had no desire to be caught into some furious dance with the cynical, judgemental, too damned seductive Broderick Kinross. She feared men who exuded such power and virility.

Rebecca moved around the massive desk, leaning against it briefly while she removed the diamond-set opal from her neck in one fluid movement. It had been wrong of her to wear it tonight. She should have risked going against Stewart's suggestion. She didn't feel proud of herself. In a sense she was a little overwhelmed by being catapulted into a world of so much obvious wealth. She had never experienced such wealth close up although she had interviewed many a celebrity with millions in her time. Sighing, Rebecca opened the top right hand drawer of Stewart's desk, placing the necklace gently inside. The light caught all the flashing lights of the large opal, sapphire, emerald, ruby, amethyst all embedded together, the dazzle of the surrounding diamonds.

It occurred to her now she really was a fool. At the far end of the drawing room, surveying the large room was a portrait of a dark-haired woman in a low-cut emerald green ball gown. Rebecca had admired it many times, knew it was Cecilia Kinross, Kimbara's first bride, painted in the early days of marriage to her kinsman, Ewan Kinross, who had taken up the great selection, the vast pastoral holding, after a big strike on the opal fields of New South Wales. Between the sumptuous gown, the beauty of the subject, the green eyes and wonderful hair, Rebecca's eyes had not dwelt on the pendant Cecilia was wearing around her neck. At first glance one could have thought the central stone was a sapphire.

She couldn't have made a bigger mistake if she tried. No wonder Liz Carol had been eyeing her so slyly every time she passed. Every guest without exception would have made the connection. There was no sense in lingering here. She would have to go back to the party.

Head bent, Rebecca turned the brass key in the lock, starting visibly when a voice addressed her from the half-open doorway.

"You know, Miss Hunt, you sure get around. So tell me what's so irresistible about my father's desk?"

Broderick Kinross pushed the heavy door open, walked into the study and stared at her.

"It was whatever was handy," she clipped. "I don't know the combination to the safe. Do *you?*"

He raised an eyebrow moving further into the room like she was a wild creature that would spring away at the first noise. "Well I might," he conceded. "Are you planning to tell how you know *exactly* where the safe is?"

She shrugged. "Your father showed it to me once. Not deliberately. I just happened to pass his study when he had the safe opened and he called me in."

He laughed, utterly amused. "You expect me to believe that?"

"Obviously not as you're looking at me like I was a first-rate con artist," Rebecca said as though she couldn't care less.

"So I ask again?" There was a gleam in his eyes. "What are you doing at my father's desk?"

"Doing what I should have done much earlier in the evening," she answered very coolly. "I'm putting the famous Necklace away."

His eyes flashed over her bare white throat. "You couldn't wait until after the party?"

She looked at him, the brilliant mocking eyes, the hard fine planes of his face, the raven shock of hair. "It's hard to imagine anyone more arrogant than you."

"Try my father," he suggested.

"*And* you don't listen when people explain. I had no idea of the significance of the Kinross Necklace. Now I know there's no way I'm going to leave it hanging around my neck." If she wanted to be safe it was time to run. Despite the fact he disliked her, a powerful attraction was running between them.

"But it's too late to undo the impact, Rebecca," he pointed out gently. "And I'm not buying your story."

"About what?" They might have been marooned together on an island.

"Women aren't the only ones to have intuition," he said. "My intuition tells me you're attracted to rich older men. I mean it could have something to do with your past life, about which we know amazingly little. You could be looking for a father figure. I studied a bit of psychology. It's textbook, Freudian stuff."

"You're talking nonsense." She broke his gaze.

"How can I be when I can see it all unfolding before my eyes."

"I'm going. I'm finding my way back." If she could get past him.

"Not for a moment." He moved like a panther to stand in front of her.

"I'll have the key if you don't mind."

She couldn't make herself touch him so he took it from her nerveless hand. "Thank you. I really ought to dare you to touch me." He inserted the key in the lock, turned it, opened the drawer, and saw the fabulous necklace within. "I wasn't accusing you of stealing it, Rebecca," he drawled.

"It hardly bothers me what you think," she answered with silky disdain.

"So why are you trembling?" He have her a faintly twisted smile, suddenly wanting to slide his hand around her creamy throat, down her neck to the delicate swell of her breast. She was small enough to pick up.

"I pride myself on behaving well," she told him. "What I'd really like to do is to take that smile off your face."

"That bad, is it?" His tone was frankly mocking. "So what are you waiting for?"

She was so affected by him she almost cried out, *Don't come near me,* instead she said with considerable control, "I think you owe me an apology."

"You're kidding me, Rebecca," he answered. "Why don't we put this in the safe? You'd better point out where it is."

She allowed herself a flash of malice. "Are you sure your father has given you the combination?"

He turned towards her, lean and powerful. "Tell me where the safe is then try me."

"Over there." She backed off, pointing. "It's behind the picture of The Hunt."

"God!" Momentarily he covered his eyes. "Dad must be losing his marbles. Come over here, Rebecca and stand by the window."

She did so borrowing some of his own mockery. "You want me to cover my eyes?"

"That's okay," he answered gently. "Just look out at the garden."

She gave a brittle little laugh. "You're really going too far, you know. Speaking to me like this."

"I don't think so," he said. "And with good reason. As a matter of fact I've been thinking about you all day."

That touched her like an electric shock. She swung about spontaneously just as he was closing the wall safe door. "I had assumed my father was well past falling in love," he said.

Her mouth curved in irony. "Did you? Then you've made an awful mistake. People fall in love at all ages. In the teens, forties, seventies, eighties. It's well documented. The great thing is *to love*."

"Listen, I agree with you." He moved with his graceful stride towards her. "Who exactly do you love, Rebecca?"

"That's hardly your business," she said shortly, but her voice shook. It seemed to her reeling mind both of them were on the edge of the utmost folly. The heavy bronze and glass chandelier overhead sculptured his handsome face with light and shade. His eyes glowed an intense sapphire simmering with arousal. He was beautiful, powerful, in the end to be feared. He could only hurt her.

"Crazy isn't it?" He echoed her depth of feeling, close to her, lifting her face to him.

Then he began to kiss her, desire overcoming every other consideration. She was too much. Too much. The pearly skin, the slender body so made for a man's loving, the sight and the scent of her. He thought he could handle it. Hell, he had followed her, all suspicion, now he enfolded her, excited by her soft cry he swiftly cut off.

Her lips were so full and soft. Like velvet. They opened to him as if she, too, had been swept away like a leaf in a storm. No woman's body had ever felt so right to him. So small yet so finely fashioned, so *yielding*. He wasn't just kissing her—he became aware of that, covering her mouth and face with a hard, hungry yearning. She was melting into him, letting him take her slight weight. It gave him the most profound shock to realise he was falling in love with this woman. This near stranger. This woman he didn't trust.

Perhaps that was what she wanted. Father and son.

The thought gave him the strength to free her, though his body was on fire.

The power she possessed. The sweetness! The mystery! All of a sudden he bitterly resented it. He had always tried to do what was right, yet he could see if he didn't hold her she might fall. Why was she doing this? How could anything work out?

"Rebecca?" he warned, the anger inside him growing as he realised he had to fight to let her go.

"What do you want me to do? Tell me?" she pleaded in a soft, husky voice. She could have wept for her own surrender when she had spent years getting her defences in order.

He stared into her face, her eyes huge and shining

with the shimmer of tears. "I shouldn't have done that," he said bleakly, thinking he should have known better. "I have to be half-mad."

There was even a possibility she was acting, witch that she was. Yet he put his hands squarely around her narrow waist and lifted her onto the desk, full of consternation that she was regarding him almost helplessly out of those beautiful eyes.

"In the bad old days, women with your powers would have run the risk of being burned at the stake," he said in a voice so mocking it splintered like wood.

"What pleasure would that have given *you?*" she retaliated, some colour coming back into her cheeks.

"Rebecca, I would have gone to your aid," he responded satirically. "No doubt about it. Probably got myself killed for my trouble."

Where was the rest of the world, he thought, wanting to kill sensation, but he couldn't. They might have been locked in some fantastic capsule.

Rebecca too was stricken. She pressed her two hands momentarily to her eyes. "I have to go back," she murmured twice like a mantra.

"I should think so." His voice had just a touch of cruelty. "Otherwise my father will be after you. Why if he found us together he could even think I'm trying to seduce you away from him."

"Except this is some nonsense you've made up. " She wrapped her arms around her.

"The tragedy is it *isn't*. You have real power in your hands, Rebecca." He reached out and lifted a handful of her long silky hair caressing it. "You even fascinate me. But there's no way I can accept your protestations of innocence. The way you've got my father eating out of your hand provides all the evidence I need.

Especially when I know him as well as I do. Here.''
Abruptly, under intense pressure, he lifted her to the
floor. ''We'd better go back but we'll take care with
our exits. You go first. I'll follow. It might come as a
big surprise but Dad has a damned expensive fireworks
display organised for you.''

''And he's done the whole thing on his own, without
reference to me.'' All of a sudden she couldn't bear to
be in the same room with him. This man who had transformed her. She felt utterly terrified of him in a sense.
Of his seductive hands and mouth, the dazzling eyes.
She had never given herself up to a man so freely. It
was prudent to take flight.

With one hand Rebecca held back her dark tumbled
hair, gesturing with the other for him to stay in place.
''I don't belong here,'' she said, seeing an end to Fee's
book, her stay on Kimbara. Everything.

''I can't make sense of it, either,'' he responded, his
white smile ironic. ''But I can tell you this and this is
the really scary bit, I can't see any of us letting you
go.''

By noon of the following day all of the guests had begun the return journey home. Rebecca who had slept
very late after a few broken hours, thought she wouldn't
have to face Brod reminding herself he was flying out
with the highly impressive Cameron brothers who were
obviously very close to him. She didn't think she could
deal with seeing Brod today but when she finally made
her way downstairs, moving quietly through the house,
she saw Stewart's study door was shut. Even from the
outside she could hear the terse sound of voices within.
Father and son in a meeting. For a split second she
wanted to race back upstairs and barricade herself in.

So he hadn't flown back to Marlu as planned? Rebecca stood motionless for a moment feeling vaguely distraught when Jean Matthews, Kimbara's housekeeper, came up behind her.

"Good morning, Rebecca. Feel like some breakfast?"

Rebecca gave a little laugh detecting the humour in the way the housekeeper said it. "Tea and toast will do, but let me get it."

"Frankly that would save me, dear," Jean Matthews said. "I'm up to my ears in work. Come back into the kitchen. I'll join you in the cuppa."

"Fee not up yet?" Rebecca asked as they walked into the marvellous old kitchen huge by any standards and outfitted for the most demanding professional chef.

"Of course not!" Jean smiled. "I expect she's nursing a little hangover. Mr. Kinross and Broderick just keep going like nothing has happened."

"I thought Brod was flying back to Marlu today," she asked trying to sound casual.

"That was my understanding." Jean nodded, putting bread in the toaster while Rebecca made the tea. "He never stays long more's the pity but I understand there's to be a meeting with Ted Holland the overseer. Between the two of us, though, Broderick and his father don't see eye to eye—everybody knows it—Broderick is in on the decision-making. Sooner or later he'll get his due."

"They're not a happy family." Rebecca gave a sigh, pouring boiling water over the fragrant best quality tea leaves in the pot.

"It didn't take you long to find that out." Jean made a wry face. "The children could have loved their father mind. They wanted to love him but he rejected it. I go way back so I know. In the old days I was Nanny. Fee tell you that? Came here when I was barely sixteen as a domestic. Still can't believe Miss Lucille has gone. She was an angel. I loved her.''

Something in her eyes conveyed she had given up trying to love her employer. ''I stayed for the children. Turn a woman's heart in her breast. I worked in the house under Mrs. Harrington, my predecessor. A real old biddy I can tell you. She used to make me so nervous, but a wonderful housekeeper and a marvellous cook. Taught me everything I know. I still remember the lessons and her superior ways. When she left Mr. Kinross asked me to take over. It's so different these days. Broderick on Marlu. Ally gone away to Sydney. Lord she could have had Rafe Cameron,'' Jean wheezed, easing her plump frame into a kitchen chair, ''but I fear it's too late. They were mad about each other but they'll never fit the pieces together again.''

Jean's eyes misted so she took off her glasses and polished them. ''Tried to talk her out of it. I know Broderick did. Rafe's his best friend. Even Mr. Kinross seemed upset.''

''It's not possible they might get together again?'' Rebecca asked, knowing that this issue had upset everyone.

''Take my word for it, luv,'' Jean sighed. ''The Camerons are very proud men.''

''No one else has got Rafe to the altar,'' Rebecca pointed out.

Jean's face brightened. ''That's true.''

Meanwhile in Stewart Kinross's study, the last thing on the agenda the decision to bid at a forthcoming auction of a well-known Central Queensland sheep and cattle station was taken. Brod went to stand up, gathering a whole sheath of papers and knocking them into shape. He'd been acutely aware his father had something on his mind he was keeping to discuss. Now it came out.

"Before you go, Brod." Stewart Kinross took off the glasses he used for reading and eased the marks on his nose, "I'd like to speak to you about what happened last night."

"I thought it was very successful," Brod said. "Everyone else did, too, going on the lavish praise."

"That wasn't the question I was about to ask." Stewart Kinross gave his son a cold stare. "Rebecca gave me to understand she asked you to put the necklace in the safe for her."

"Indeed she did. You were busy with guests at the time. She couldn't wait to take the darn thing off, though you'd never have known it. Cool as a cucumber, Rebecca."

"Can we be serious for a moment?" Stewart Kinross snapped.

"What do you want me to say, Dad?" Brod turned back. "Under the porcelain exterior she's one tough little cookie."

"Rebecca, tough? I hope you haven't been saying anything to offend her?"

"Would I do that, Dad?" Brod asked, trying to keep his temper.

"You take particular pleasure in stirring people up. What I want to know is did you find a way to make her feel uncomfortable in the necklace?"

"*I* find a way?" Brod slapped his handful of papers down on the massive desk again. "As it turned out,

Dad, *you* did that. Given that the Necklace and its history is well-known, I would have thought any young woman would have found it awkward to wear. It is intended, as we all know, for my future wife.''

Stewart Kinross shot back his huge swivelled leather chair. "Are you suggesting I'm way too old to consider remarrying?"

"God, Dad." Brod struck his fist into his hand. "I wouldn't have shed a tear if you'd married half a dozen of the women you've had in the past. Some of them were actually nice. But Rebecca Hunt is way off limits." The very thought burned him up.

Stewart Kinross smiled bleakly. "You've obviously led too isolated a life, Brod. Is it her age, twenty-seven you're getting at?"

Brod turned fully to face his father, his lean, powerful young-man frame crackling with energy. "Dad, she's too *young*. She's only a little bit older than Ally. She's younger than *I* am."

"So?" Stewart Kinross's face might have been carved out of rock. "I don't see that puts too much of a barrier in my way."

Brod sat down hard. "So you're really serious about this?"

Stewart Kinross's handsome face coloured. "She's exactly the sort of woman I've always looked for."

"You mean damned secretive?" Brod flared. "Even if she were in her forties you'd have to know more about her."

"I know enough," Stewart Kinross thundered. "I can understand your fears, Brod. Rebecca is young enough to want children."

"Well of course! Have you even *begun* to discuss

this? It doesn't seem likely. Rebecca told me she had no idea of the significance of the Necklace. She wore it because she didn't wish to offend you. You were pretty insistent."

Stewart Kinross seemed to take a long time to answer. "You weren't there at the time, Brod."

God, *had* she lied to him? Brod thought bitterly.

"Of course I told Rebecca the whole story," his father answered emphatically. "Damned silly of me not to have. With people like you around someone was bound to tell her."

Brod wondered if he could take it in. "You told her it has only been worn by Kinross *wives?* That my mother was the last woman to wear it?"

Stewart Kinross shrugged. "Well I never mentioned your mother, Brod. I haven't spoken about your mother in many long years. She behaved very badly. She left me and you children. She broke her sacred vows and she was punished."

A look of furious distaste crossed Brod's face. "What a cold-blooded bastard you are," he said with profound resentment. "Punished, my God! My poor mother. If only I'd been older! She could have married just about anyone else. Some normal guy and she'd be alive to this day."

Stewart Kinross's eyes were as cold as ice. "Then you'd never have been what passes for my heir."

"I am your heir, Dad. Never forget it." Brod's face hardened to granite, his gaze so formidable his father was forced to look away.

"Well I think that's all," Stewart decided somewhat hastily. "You seem to think I'm not entitled to some life of my own, Brod. That being fifty-five I should scale down all my expectations."

Brod moved to the door, feeling shaken now. Rebecca had *lied* to him. "I've never known you to scale down on anything, Dad. You think you're Royalty. Money isn't a consideration. If I weren't so damned efficient you'd have to be more careful about how you're getting rid of so much of it."

The fact it was true put Stewart Kinross on the defensive. "I can't imagine who you think you're talking to," he blustered. "I'm your father."

"Damned right you are," Brod answered grimly, "and a pretty miserable one at that."

"I think you'd better go now," his father warned. "I don't need any lectures on my sins as a parent. Truth is you're jealous of me, Brod. You always have been. Now there's Rebecca…" Stewart Kinross paused, staring at his son. "I've tried to stop thinking about you two last night. Some expression on your faces when you were dancing."

Brod gave an abrupt laugh and rubbed his chiselled chin. "Keeping an eye on us were you, Dad?"

"I made a bad decision last time," his father said. "One I don't intend to make again. I have to confess I was a little disappointed in Rebecca. You seem to disturb her. About what, I wonder? Did you threaten her?"

"To put it bluntly, Dad. I let her know it wouldn't be a good idea to get mixed up with you." It only struck him afterwards that hadn't been the smart thing to say. He should have let his father believe he and Rebecca were attracted. Hell weren't they? No matter what he thought of her. For now he had to get out of the house. He didn't think he could handle meeting up with Miss Rebecca Hunt without blowing his top. Grant wasn't due to pick him up until the following afternoon. He'd go join Ted, Kimbara's overseer. Take a good look around the station as they had already discussed. A good man, Ted. He had hand-picked him himself.

Fee didn't feel up to working, preferring to spend most of the day "resting" so Rebecca continued with her own research. When she called in on Fee she implored her to tell her all about Cecilia's Necklace. Free, holding a hand to her throbbing temples, told her where to look.

"The library, darling. The bookcase to the left of the fireplace. Near the sofa. The middle section as I recall. It's all there."

"Sure I can't get you something, Fee?" Rebecca asked. The older woman was wearing a little make-up, she was never without it, but she looked decidedly under the weather.

"My youth back, darling," Fee called.

It was a very large library indeed. One of the finest private libraries in the country with thousands of leather-bound volumes and records going back to the earliest days of settlement. It was an important room in the house. Rebecca felt privileged to be there. She loved books with a passion. The look of them, the feel of them, the smell, all the wonder, the information, the excitement and wisdom they contained. Following Fee's directions she discovered the small leather-bound volume, with gold tooling published in the early 1870s giving an account of the Kinross-Cameron opal strike. Rebecca settled into the deep comfortable sofa, shifted a few piled-up cushions then began to turn the yellowing pages.

An hour later she was still reading. The adventurous young Ewan Kinross and his equally adventurous friend Charles Cameron, second and third sons respectively of good family had left Scotland in the mid-1800s to make their fortunes on the Australian gold fields. They hadn't succeeded in panning gold, not really knowing enough about it, but they persevered with their mining interests, all the time learning from the more experienced miners talk, until they were eventually rewarded by discovering a rich opal bearing seam southwest of the town on Rinka in New South Wales.

They took out a lease despite being told their find was probably worthless. The rest was history. The mine, Kinross-Cameron, gave up magnificent stones and made the men rich. Rich enough to do what they always wanted: take up adjoining great selections in far South West Queensland and raise the finest beef cattle in the land.

One particularly beautiful stone was kept to be made into a pendant for Ewan's kinswoman, Cecilia Drummond. Both young men were in love with her and the pendant was by way of showing their deep regard for her. The story was that both young men settled into trying to win her hand, adding a new dimension *rivalry* to their close friendship. It appeared at times Charles Cameron was the more favoured of the two. Indeed a family letter suggested Charles was her "knight in shining armour." But in the end Cecilia made her choice marrying Ewan Kinross and giving him four children.

Reading between the lines it appeared the marriage was not a happy one. Perhaps Cecilia would have done better to marry Charles. For a while it seemed the friendship between the two men was almost ruined then after the birth of Cecilia's first child things appeared to come right again. Charles Cameron in fact was one of the godparents.

Rebecca closed the book, leaning back into the sofa.

Impossible to believe Stewart hadn't told her the full story. When she looked at the photograph of Lucille Kinross in full evening dress wearing the pendant Rebecca had almost felt the tears coming. She'd had no right wearing the necklace last night. Brod would never forgive her for it even if he could accept she had no knowledge of the pendant's significance.

She knew now Brod had gone out for the day with Ted Holland. He hadn't bothered with lunch at the homestead so she wouldn't see him again until dinner. Fee had already told her she was going to make an effort to get up.

"I see too little of my nephew," she said. "I could scarcely get near him last night for that Carol girl. I think she actually fears letting go of his arm."

Even so Liz Carol hadn't been able to keep Brod to herself. Rebecca, without appearing to notice, had seen him dancing with a number of pretty girls.

When she stood up to replace the volume on the shelf Stewart Kinross, impressive in his riding clothes, came to the door.

"How you do manage to lose yourself, Rebecca," he said, smiling rather fiercely. "I've been looking for you everywhere."

"It's a big house, Stewart," she pointed out mildly. "In fact the biggest private house I've ever been in outside of English stately homes."

"Now you're talking!" he said. "This would be a modest cottage compared to over there."

"This could never be a modest cottage anywhere," Rebecca said dryly. "There's something I wanted to talk to you about anyway, Stewart."

"Marvellous." He threw that off. "First get started

on changing into your riding clothes. I feel like a good gallop. Get all that party feeling out of my system.''

Rebecca resisted. ''You don't think there might be an afternoon storm.'' She was a little scared of storms. ''It's turned very hot.''

''There could be I guess,'' he conceded, ''but nothing to worry us. I've seen the most monumental storm clouds blow up. Great masses of purplish clouds rolling across the desert. But not one drop of rain. Before long a wind gets up and the clouds are blown asunder. If you get dressed I'll go down to the stables and organise the horses. If you're a particularly good girl I'll let you put Jeeba through her paces.''

He turned and was gone, leaving Rebecca to climb the central staircase and find her way back to her room. Although it was so quiet, the day seemed to be thrumming with a strange kind of electricity. It was only when she was dressed in her riding gear, standing on the front verandah putting on her hat, that she took time to really examine the enamelled blue sky.

At the moment all seemed to be well, yet for some reason she had lightning on her mind. She and a friend had been caught once sailing in his yacht, one of the scariest experiences she had had. They were miles from anywhere with lightning flashing closer every time and the ninety-six-foot mast soaring to the lowering sky like a giant lightning rod. Her friend Simon had told her to get inside the cabin and disconnect the aerials and the power leads. If the worst came to the worst and the yacht was struck, at least the radio would still be working. She had never to this day forgotten the experience even though the storm passed over them without incident.

*   *   *

They rode southwards along a chain of tranquil billabongs where the River Red gums gave shade with their
wonderful abundance of fresh green foliage. None of
the pools was deep at this time though these same pools,
Rebecca had been told, could flood miles beyond their
banks. Stewart had pointed out flood debris caught high
up in the branches of these riverside trees, indicating
the height the floods had reached. A flat-topped mesa a
few miles off looked remarkable in the brilliant afternoon light. It rose from the burnt umber plains to glow
fiery red against the sky so blue it had turned violet.

The mirage, too, was abroad, creating such strange
atmospheric tricks. It seemed to Rebecca's dazzled eyes
a nomadic tribe was travelling across the landscape but
the closer they rode the further off these wraithlike people appeared until they finally disappeared.

The desert birds most active early morning or getting
on towards sunset were out in their countless thousands,
their trilling and shrieking filling the air. Rebecca had
often felt sorry for little budgerigars in a cage; now she
rejoiced in the sight of them in the wild. They flew in
great numbers across the increasingly incandescent sky,
the dancing light throwing up vivid flashes of emerald-
green from the wings and gold from the head and neck.
Down in the lignum swamps nested the great colonies
of Ibis. Kimbara was a major breeding ground for nomadic water birds, the spoonbills, the egrets and herons,
the countless thousands of ducks and water hens. The
pelicans stuck to the remoter swamps while the beautifully plumaged parrots, the pink and grey galahs and
the white corellas tended to favour the mulga.

As they rode the trail back up to the grassy flats
topped with tiny purple flowers in their millions
Stewart, crouched low in the saddle, challenged her to

a race. She took after him giving her spirited chestnut mare, Jeeba, all the encouragement she needed. It was hopeless; Stewart was by far the better rider and the big bay gelding he was riding much stronger and speedier than the mare. It should have, but it didn't seem to chase the cobwebs away. Rebecca was starting to feel quite alarmed by the sky. She stopped short near a clump of bauhinia trees and turned in the saddle, grey eyes anxious. "Stewart don't you think we should be heading back?"

He reined in beside her, reaching over to put a hand over hers. "Why so nervous, my dear?"

She withdrew her hand very gently pretending to adjust her cream Akubra. "I'm not normally nervous but the storm doesn't seem to be all that far away. Look at the sky."

"Goodness I've seen worse," he responded a little tersely, watching her start as a cockatoo nearby gave an agonised screech. "I know all about these things, my dear. I might look like a Wagnerian holocaust but we've been in drought."

"Well if that's what you think," she said doubtfully, still eyeing the lurid sky.

"So now's a good time to ask me what you wanted to earlier," Stewart suggested.

Rebecca decided to tackle the issue head-on not duck it. "I expect you know what it is, Stewart," she said. "I didn't have the slightest idea the Necklace you lent me was so important to the family. Why didn't you tell me?"

He gave her the look of a man who thinks himself insulted. "My dear I don't usually do things accompanied by an explanation."

"I think in this case you might have made an exception,'' she said very seriously. ''I understand the Necklace was last worn by your wife.''

His jaw tightened perceptibly. ''Rebecca, that's no big secret. What is bothering you *exactly?* I saw you and Brod together last night. Did he take it upon himself to correct you for wearing it?''

''Not at all.'' Rebecca met his gaze. On no account was she going to create more discord between father and son.

''Please tell me,'' he urged, as though reading her thoughts. ''Don't hold anything back.''

She saw a flash of lightning appear on the horizon. ''Stewart, it's a very beautiful necklace,'' Rebecca said, realising she was struggling with anxiety, ''but it didn't make me happy to know it's promised to Brod's future wife.''

Steward Kinross gave an icy chuckle. ''My dear it belongs to *me* until such time. More to the point I could remarry. I've a damned lot to offer.''

''I'm sure you have, Stewart.'' Rebecca felt she was floundering out of her depth. ''It's just that it wasn't right to lend it to *me.*''

He hesitated, the grimness of his expression gentling. ''You look like you're about to cry.''

She set off deliberately. ''I assure you I'm not. I think it has something to do with the colour of my eyes. You wouldn't believe the number of people who've told me that.''

''They shimmer like diamonds.'' The look he flashed at her contained such a degree of feeling Rebecca, at that moment, felt she didn't have the strength to confront it. But she had to face the fact Stewart's infatuation with her had ruined things completely. If she didn't leave Kimbara, where would it all end?

"I really feel, Stewart, we have to get out of here," she urged, her face showing her strain. "The lightning seems to be getting closer."

He peered almost nonchalantly at the sort of sky he had seen countless times in his life. "My dear, it's many kilometres away. But if you're frightened..."

She felt no shame. "It's only reasonable to take precautions. I wouldn't like to be caught out in the open."

He continued to sit the big bay, silently staring at her. "You don't feel anything for me, do you?" he said eventually, his handsome face hard and flat.

She was almost too unnerved to speak. "Stewart, this is all a mistake," she cried. "I have to go."

"It's because of Broderick, isn't it?" He appeared to force out the words.

"Stewart, that's an insane idea," she protested, laying a calming hand on Jeeba's neck.

"Is it?"

The way he said it made her hair crawl on her scalp. "And you've no right to ask." She'd had enough bullying to last her a lifetime.

"There's no way I'll let him have you." He made a grab for her reins but Rebecca was waiting. She kicked a boot into Jeeba's side and the mare, already on the nervous side, responded by tearing off, its flying hooves crushing all the little wildflowers and scattering tufts of grass.

God was there no way out of this! Was she doomed to fire men's sexual obsession?

Rebecca let the mare gallop furiously across the valley, heading the startled animal towards the long broad hollow like a trench at the edge of a treeless slope. They had passed it on the ride out. There was a shorter time now between the lightning flash and the thunder. The lightning was coming closer. Why ever had Stewart chosen to take the horses out? They were so very exposed there seemed like no escape. He had put them at risk? She started to pray for the rain to come down so it could soak her to the skin. Much safer to have wet clothes when lightning was about. Any charge would conduct through the wet clothes rather than the body. She didn't even know if Stewart was far behind her.

Aware of the approaching storm, Brod headed back early to the homestead parking the Jeep in the drive. He worked his way through the house, saw nobody, then went to Fee's room, tapping on the door.

"Fee, it's me," he called. "Where's everyone?"

Fee, who had been lightly dozing, pulled herself off the bed and went to the door. "Hello there, darling. I've been catching up on my beauty sleep."

"Where's Dad and Rebecca?" he asked, sounding mighty taut.

"Are they missing?" Fee blinked.

"There's no one about."

Reluctantly Fee pulled herself wide-awake. "Ah yes, I know. Rebecca did come to the door to tell me they were going riding."

"When was this?" Brod frowned.

"Oh, darling, I'd say a couple of hours ago. What is it?" Fee, catching his mood, asked with a thread of apprehension.

"They're not home, unless they've arrived back at the stables. There's one hell of a storm about to break, Fee. It's been threatening all afternoon. Dad knows the risks of taking the horses out on a day like this."

Fee's mouth turned down. "You know your father, dear. He likes playing God."

"He's got Rebecca with him," Brad clipped off. "I'm really surprised he decided to take her out riding. For that matter couldn't *she* look up and see the sky?"

"For that matter I haven't seen it myself," Fee only half joked, darting away to the verandah. "Good Lord!" she breathed, reading the extraordinary sky. Her demeanour changed, becoming very serious. "That's pretty alarming even by our standards." She looked up at Brod who had joined her. "I'm sure they're safe, darling," she offered, recognising his deep concern. "My guess is they're taking shelter in the caves."

His lean face darkened. "Only a fool would head out that way today. They're more likely to have taken the Willowie trail. I'm going after them."

Fee put a detaining hand on his arm. "Be careful, darling, your father won't like that."

"A pity!" he rasped. "This is a disaster, Fee. The whole business. Dad's acting like a complete fool."

"He's only human, Brod," Fee said quietly, though sometimes in the past she had wondered if it were true.

"He told me this morning he explained all about the Necklace to Rebecca. Still she wore it."

He sounded so violently outraged, so betrayed, Fee had no hesitation speaking her mind. "I suppose you've considered your father could have been lying, Brod. I know that girl."

He turned away urgently. "Maybe she's making fools of us all. I don't know. For the first time in my life I don't *know*. But I'm going after her because I do know Dad. If anything goes wrong she won't be able to handle him."

He drove fast across the valley, cursing beneath his breath as the lightning flashes grew closer, followed in long seconds by the deafening crash of thunder. He estimated the lightning was only a couple of kilometres away. Whatever had possessed his father to ride out on such an afternoon? Was he full of hope if he had Rebecca alone he could convince her he cared for her? That he knew she could come to care about him? That he could cocoon her in a world of luxury? Had he even been heading towards the caves knowing at some point in the afternoon they would have to take shelter? Well he had no right to do it, Brod fumed. No right to harass her. Or was this what she wanted all along?

He didn't know the truth. He was only guessing.

Another brilliant flash of lightning forked from the clouds to the ground. Instinctively he winced. When he reopened his eyes it was to see a horse and rider galloping full tilt across the illuminated landscape with another rider hot in pursuit. He could see the first rider was a woman. She had lost her hat and her long hair was flying like a silk banner on the wind.

Rebecca! Whatever she was, saint or sinner, he felt relief pour into his body. He swung the Jeep in her direction. She appeared to be making for the deep depression that ran like a curving gully around the base of the nearest hillock. At least she had some sense. No one in their right mind would take shelter beneath a tree. The first big drops were falling now, striking the hard ground. This was the time of greatest risk.

Just as he thought it, suddenly, violently as though waiting for the exact moment to find its victim, a bolt of lightning was flung down from the leaden clouds casting a terrifying blaze before it forked into the second rider with a glow that burned the retina.

Almost blinded, caged in the Jeep, Brod felt such shock, such pain, it was almost as if his own heart had stopped. His father had been struck before his very eyes. Not only the man, horse and rider were down. Now came the inevitable clap of thunder, like the roar of some malevolent god, deeper, darker, devastating the ears. He could see Rebecca had become unseated, a small huddle on the ground, while Jeeba was struggling to her feet.

He felt compelled to go to Rebecca first. Drag her into the Jeep where she would be safer than anywhere else. Then he had to go to his father. He knew as well as anybody, lightning can and did strike more than once in the same place but he had to go all the same. His eyes stung behind his narrowed lids, as his whole life seemed to crowd in on him. He realised at that moment the whole day had blazed in an excess of strangeness and the threat of danger.

Rebecca was fully conscious, moaning a little. He ran his hands over her swiftly—he was certain no bones were broken then he lifted her high in his arms bundling her into the Jeep.

"Brod? My God, what happened?"

"Lightning, a lightning strike," he shouted. "Stay in the Jeep. Don't move." He slammed the door shut, enraged and saddened to see Jeeba tottering in pain. If she'd broken a leg she would have to be put down. Now inexplicably the ferocity of the storm abated, seeming to pass directly over them towards the eroded chain of hills with its network of caves.

He found his father on the now sodden ground, the big bay gelding dead beneath him. Desperately keeping his emotions in check he began massage and mouth-to-mouth resuscitation, stopping for a minute, starting again.

At some point Rebecca joined him, ghostly pale, her

hair streaming water, looking so young she might have been home from boarding school.

"Brod," she said very gently, after a while, taking his arm, holding it, letting her head come to rest against his shoulder. "Your father is dead."

"What are you talking about?" he defied her. "He's living, breathing…"

"Brod, he's not."

Even so he had to make his last-ditch attempt, knowing beside him Rebecca was crying. "He can't be dead," he said, sounding so definite when he knew all life had fled.

"I'm so sorry…so sorry…" Rebecca crumpled as though all her energy had been burnt up. This had to be the worst day of her life. Such a dreadful thing for Brod. She wanted to comfort him, only exhaustion conquered her.

Now from everywhere men converged on the scene, pushing onwards until they reached the spot where Stewart Kinross lay dead on the ground, his son bowed over him holding his head in his hands. Rebecca was huddled in the grass, motionless though her lips were moving in prayer.

"What in the name of God has happened here?" Ted Holland demanded in the utmost confusion. "Brod, speak to me, man."

Slowly Brod turned up his head. "My father did something incredibly foolish, Ted. He rode out in an electrical storm. I saw the lightning hit him. I saw him go down, his horse under him. Both of them were struck."

"Lord God and the little lady?" Ted stared at Rebecca who appeared quite calm but disoriented.

"I'm afraid she's in shock," Brod said bleakly. "We'll have to get her back to the house. Get her warm. A shot of something. Fee is there, Ted. Take the Jeep then come back for me. I have to get my father home."

CHAPTER FIVE

ALISON KINROSS received the news of her father's death when she was attending a party given for a visiting American film star.

"Take it in the study, Ally," her society hostess murmured, drawing her gently aside. "It's your brother."

There had to be a very good reason for Brod to go to these lengths to track her down, Ally thought, immediately panicked. She and Brod spoke often on the phone but if he didn't find her at home he always left a message on the machine. She hurried into the Sinclair study and shut the door after her. She was a strikingly beautiful young woman with a mane of dark curly hair and almond-shaped green eyes. Family eyes. Fiona Kinross had them, always using them to great effect.

"He's dead, Ally," Brod said very quietly when she picked up the receiver and identified herself. "Our father was killed in a lightning strike this afternoon."

She didn't cry though it was the last thing she had been expecting to hear. Her father had hurt her too badly over the years for tears but she felt a tremendous grief for what might have been. "Where, Brod? How?"

She listened while Brod told what had happened. Not *exactly* what had happened. How his father had invited Rebecca to ride with him when he obviously knew a lot better. Unless as Brod suspected his father had some plan of his own in mind. That was a large part of the way his father had worked. Hidden agendas. Besides, he never had introduced the subject of his father's infatuation with Rebecca Hunt to Ally. He wasn't going to. Not *now*. Though Ally would hear of it. He was certain of that. He continued to talk, his tone grave and quiet

"I'll come," Ally said finally. "I'll fly out in the morning." She struggled with the thought of what it was all going to mean.

"Charter a flight," Brod advised her. "Just get here quickly."

"I love you, Brod," she said. Brod her powerful big brother. The brother who had always looked out for her and treated her with such affection.

"I love you, too, Ally." His vibrant voice was subdued. "I can't imagine how we're going to get through this, but we will."

When Ally put the phone down a moment later, she was conscious of the trembling right through her body. The party was over for her. She would make her excuses to her hosts then go home and pack.

The end of an era she thought. The beginning of Brod's reign.

As she walked to the tall double doors of the study, the light caught the lustrous gleam of her strapless emerald dress. There would be many difficulties ahead, she thought, not the least of them having to see Rafe again. Her father's funeral would be big. He'd been—dear Lord the past tense—an important man. Members of most Outback families would be there. Politicians, the legal fraternity, businesspeople. The Cameron brothers would be singled out as close family friends. The old gossip would circulate. Everybody knew of her love affair with Rafe. Hadn't she gloried in it? But in the end, overcome by the sheer tempestuousness of their feelings, she had run away. She had run like her mother and Rafe, her beloved Rafe, had wiped his hands of her. The very thought of him might still fill her with longing but she knew she had lost him forever.

When Fee rang her daughter, Francesca, in London she never expected Francesca to tell her, "I'm coming, Fee. I'll book a flight as soon as I get off the phone. I know you and Uncle Stewart had your differences. I know *why* but he was always very nice to me. It's the very least I can do. Besides, I'm longing to see you and the family, Brod and Ally." It seemed a far too inappropriate time to mention Grant Cameron even when his golden unashamedly macho image kept popping into her mind at the oddest times. Like someone you can't possibly forget.

"The funeral is on Friday," Fee was saying. "My poor brother in a cold room but it will give Brod the time to make all the arrangements. I can tell you everyone is shocked out of their minds. Not a lot of people have liked Stewart. A lot feared him. But he had such vigour. Surely he can't be dead."

"I can't really take it in, either," Francesca confessed distressed, sweeping her hair back off her forehead. "So now Brod is master of Kimbara. He's taken over the inheritance he was born for."

"Kimbara will be a different place," Fee vowed. "Though it grieves me to say it, Stewart served himself. Brod is like my darling, Sir Andy. He'll serve his heritage."

"It's so sad about Ally and Brod," Francesca said, depressed by her own intimate knowledge of family matters and the lack of love.

"Do you think I don't realise what *you* missed,

Francesca,'' Fee asked with a pang. "I was a terrible mother.''

Francesca couldn't help nodding. "I know!" She gave a kind little laugh, then sobered. "But I love you.''

"I know and I don't deserve it.'' Fee cleared her throat.'' I couldn't feel more comfort knowing you're coming. Such a long flight! I want you to meet Rebecca. She was out riding with Stewart when he was struck so she's taking it very hard. In fact she wants to leave.''

"Well I can understand it,'' Francesca breathed. "It must have been awful for her.''

"Just like Stewart to go and do something dreadfully dramatic,'' Fee wailed. "Let me know your flight, dearest. We'll organise a connecting charter flight. Maybe that marvellous hunk Grant Cameron could pick you up. He's sure to want to meet you again.''

I hope! Francesca thought, breaking the connection. She looked up from the bed where she'd been sitting to catch sight of her reflection in the pier mirror. She looked nothing like her beautiful mother. She took after her father's side of the family. She had a cousin, Alexandra, with the same red-gold hair and flower-blue eyes. People often mistook them for sisters.

The quintessential English Rose, Grant Cameron had called her with amused admiration, but with the suspicion her beauty and strength would be sapped in the harsh environment of the Outback.

Maybe just maybe, he didn't know enough about her.

Rebecca, who had sought refuge in a lovely cool seating area on the far reaches of the garden, lifted her head at the sound of footsteps on the gravel path. Hurriedly she tried to smooth the marks of tears from her face. Stewart's sudden violent death had hit her terribly hard, the shock compounded by feelings of guilt as though her rejection of him had somehow led to his death. It was irrational. She knew that, but it didn't help. It was Stewart who had made the dreadful mistake of not seeking protection for both of them yet her part in the tragedy weighed heavily on her.

Fee had given her the news Ally and Francesca were both coming for the funeral. Both intended to stay for a time. There was no place for her here with the family arriving, though Fee had been quick to beg her to stay. The footsteps grew louder. A man's footsteps.

Brod's. He was coming towards her, more formally dressed than usual as different people were flying in all the time to express their condolences and lend their support. Rebecca had never thought to see roses blooming so prolifically in the Outback yet now he passed under a double arch aglow with large yellow roses. Soon he would reach her.

Rebecca drew a deep, shaky breath, not fully understanding her own powerful reactions to the man. Both of them had made it their business to avoid each other. Now he had come to seek her out. For what reason? To ask her to leave? Innocent of all blame she regarded it as only natural. She threw aside a cushion, standing up as though readying herself for a verdict.

"Don't hurry away, Rebecca," he said, as good as blocking the narrow path with his tall, wide-shouldered frame. His tone was crisp but not unfriendly.

"What is it, Brod?" she asked without further hesitation, unhappily aware her voice was husky.

"I thought it was about time we had a little talk." He stored up the sight of her in his mind. "I haven't bothered you. I'm sympathetic to your shock but I want to know what happened yesterday."

It was so quiet only for the sound of the birds. She felt trapped.

"I can't talk about it, Brod," she said and turned away from him urgently, as he moved into the leafy garden sanctuary. She wanted comfort. She felt this man could have given it, except he had locked his mind and his heart against her.

"You *will* tell me, Rebecca," he warned quietly. "You owe it to me." He put out a hand not to restrain her but to turn her to face him. "Tears. Lots of tears. For my father?" She looked hurt like a child, her womanly powers of seduction not sending the usual messages from her beautiful drowned eyes.

"I can't help think I was somehow to blame."

Her voice was so deeply pained he found himself trying to ease it. "My father knew to seek shelter, Rebecca." He stared at her, trying to read her mind. "But I'm surprised you consented to go with him. Surely you could see a major storm was building up?"

She sat down again, with him towering over her, locking her hands tightly to calm herself. "I didn't want to go, Brod, but your father made it seem the tremendous build up of storm clouds was no more than some grand celestial display. He didn't expect a single drop of rain to fall."

Damn it! Dad and his tricks. "That *can* happen," he explained, "but my father could read the different skies as well as I can." He knew he would be too close to her to sit on the padded bench, her graceful body only inches from his, so he moved back a little to sit on the low stone wall surrounding a raised bed of flowers. "I want you to tell me where you were headed?" he asked.

She looked up briefly, grey eyes dominating her pale

face. "Your father was going to show me the aboriginal rock paintings in the caves."

His suspicions confirmed. "He said that, did he?" he asked bleakly.

"I didn't really want to see them." Even then she vehemently shook her head. "I mean I do want to see them, but I'd been feeling so anxious all day. Now I know why."

"So you didn't manage to get that far?" he persisted with his line of thought.

"Put it this way—" she shrugged "—I kept heading in a different direction. Along the chain of billabongs. I love all the water lilies and the bird life."

"What are you hiding, Rebecca?" he asked all of a sudden, very blunt.

"What is it you think I should say," she pleaded. "I have to live with this."

God only knows what happened, he thought, sick to death of it all. "You sound distraught."

"I am." Her shadowed eyes flashed. "I want to go home."

He found he was violently opposed to that. "You're not a child. You're a woman and you have professional commitments." He said the first thing that came into his head.

"Your family is coming." She spread her elegant hands. "All your friends. I have no place here."

His eyes blazed. "You've made quite a place for yourself, though, haven't you, Rebecca. Did my father tell you he was in love with you?" He wanted desperately to know what had gone on.

"What does any of it matter, Brod?" She turned her face away from him.

"That means he *did*."

"I don't know what he was saying," she evaded, when she would never forget.

"Don't give me that. *Please*. He was so caught up with you." The dappled sunshine fell over his taut face. "You knew it."

"I learned it the hard way." Now she almost gave herself away.

"How?" he rasped.

"Your father never touched me," she whispered, a little shocked by his expression.

"All right," he answered. "Calm down. But he said something to send you galloping madly away."

"And that's when it happened," she sighed deeply, "the tragedy. I don't want to talk about it any more."

"The thing is, Rebecca, there are consequences for our actions," he pointed out. "Look at me and tell me you didn't intend for my father to fall in love with you?" Hardness broke through his quiet tone, cruelly cutting her.

"What difference would it make?" She flew up and turned fully to face him, finding the very air was suffocating. "You believe what you want to believe."

He caught her shoulders, smelling her fragrance. "That's a cop-out really, isn't it?"

"I don't want to quarrel with you, Brod," she said, locked into his magnetism.

Now the woman sprang to vibrant life. He saw it flare out of her eyes, wrapping them both in a desperate hunger. "Well tell me what you do want?" he asked harshly, his thumbs moulding her delicate collar-bones.

"I want to forget I ever met you," she heard herself saying. God knows he was out to hurt her. "I want to forget all of this."

"All of *what?*" he asked forcefully, feeling she was

stealing something from him. His self-control. "I thought you were set on marrying a Kinross. You don't care which one?"

As antiviolent as it was possible for a woman to be, Rebecca, driven beyond her normal behaviour, threw back her hand intending to slap his beautiful, hateful face only he caught her wrist in mid-air, overwhelming her with his strength. His eyes flashed danger. "Tell me what you came here for, Rebecca? The biography was only the start. When did you decide there was a great deal more on offer?"

She could hear and see the tumult that was going on in him. Tumult that was heating her own blood. "Go on, lash out at me if it can help you through it," she cried, pushing against him with trembling hands. "I know I hate you."

"Ah, yes." He narrowed his eyes. "We've already discovered that." He brought her face up to him with insistent fingers, lowering his head to claim her mouth, while she in agony of mixed emotions tried to offer resistance.

Flames danced around them, locking them in a dangerous circle.

"You drive me mad," he muttered, as his lips finally left hers.

"I'm going home, Brod." Incredibly she leaned her head against his chest. She had to be crazy. Only he was so physically perfect to her she didn't know if she could possibly withstand him.

"Where's home?" Now he was absorbed in kissing her throat and she was letting him do it, allowing passion to convulse her.

"Away from you." Her voice broke with emotion.

"I don't believe that." He gave a little laugh, something like triumph in the sound. ''God, I don't believe what I'm doing myself. Is this a plan or are we just part of a pattern. Destiny if you will. You know my father brought you to this place?''

She grew very still within his arms, touched all over with alarm. ''What are saying, Brod?''

''He never told you himself?'' He lifted his head to stare into her eyes.

Now she had her free will back. ''I weep for you, Brod,'' she said stormily. ''For the sad life you've led. You can't trust anyone, can you?''

''I trust lots of people,'' he proclaimed. ''But not a magnolia so white and pure. There's much too much mystery to you for that.''

Some relationships are ruined before they start. ''I'm going up to the house to pack,'' Rebecca said, disgust in her eyes.

''Won't do you much good.'' He gave a little shrug. ''I'll take the pledge not to ask you too many tough questions but you're staying, Rebecca, make no mistake about that. No one will fly you out without my say-so and you owe it to my father to attend his funeral. You admitted as much yourself.''

Alison arrived mid-afternoon, tired from the journey but thrilled to be home on Kimbara. It still exerted a powerful influence on her.

Her eyes filled with tears at the sight of her brother. Although they talked often, she hadn't seen that much of Brod in the past few years, now his striking maturity and the enhanced presence of his inheritance was fully revealed to her. It occurred to her suddenly Brod had a decided look of Sir Andy about him. A quality their father by no means had had. She remembered that look of Sir Andy's well. Brod had it, too. The high mettled pride. Not the arrogance but the pride of real achievement.

"Ally, it's wonderful to see you." Brod gathered his sister into a huge hug, fighting down the impulse to tell her she was much too thin. "I only wish it were happier times." Still holding her hand he led her to the Jeep. "Climb in. I'll take care of your luggage. I sure hope you're going to stay for a while like you promised."

"It's wonderful to know I can," she called back.

No more arguments with her father. No more stepping into the combat zone. No more scathing condemnation for not marrying Rafe.

"I don't suppose you were worthy of him anyway." The contemptuous words still rang in her ears. Years later.

It wasn't what one expected to hear from one's father.

Her few pieces of luggage loaded away, Brod got behind the wheel. "Fran is due in tomorrow. I've organised with Grant to pick her up at Longreach. I'd go for her myself, I guess I can call the Beech Baron my own, only so many people have been flying in and out paying their respects."

"I wonder if it's more wanting to offer you support than mourning Dad," Ally said bleakly, looking out the window at the vastness of the land. Kimbara was another world. "Dad had no idea how to make friends of people."

"That was his misfortune," Brod said gravely. "There was something I wanted to talk to you about before we got up to the house." He was worried Ally might hear it from someone else. "You know about Rebecca, of course."

Ally gave him a sharp look from her clear green eyes.

"What is that supposed to mean?" she asked in wonderment. "I thought Rebecca was here to write Fee's biography. Fee speaks highly of her. Obviously they've hit it off."

Brod's chiselled profile was serious. "They have but there's a little more to it than that. It will come as a shock to you but Dad was utterly infatuated with her." It had to be in the genes.

Ally blinked her astonishment. "What?" Her voice cracked. "Could Dad be infatuated with any woman? I hate to say this but I never thought he liked women at all. Not after our mother left."

"There were women in his life. You know that." Brod gave her a brief sidelong glance.

"True," Ally conceded, "but he never married one of them."

"I think he was beginning to see Rebecca in that light," Brod told her grimly. "She's very beautiful in just the way he liked. Cool, poised, patrician. Someone who could easily take over the role of his wife."

"For God's sake." Ally turned her head to study her brother's face. "I thought she was my age or thereabouts?"

"Ally, you'd be familiar with rich men marrying younger women," he countered.

"But Fee hasn't said a word about this," Ally protested, having difficulty taking it in. Her father thinking of remarrying. Now he was dead!

"Fee doesn't want to think about it." Brod said bluntly. "I wouldn't be mentioning it myself only chances are someone will tell you at the funeral, human nature being what it is. The real problem was Dad lent Rebecca Cecilia's Necklace to wear at the function the other night."

"Brod!" Ally looked her shock. "In that case, we could have a little gold digger right under our noses. She must have known."

His handsome mouth tightened. "I'm by no means certain of that. Rebecca says he didn't tell her. Fee believes her."

"And you? Why the doubt?"

Brod put a hand to his temple. "I can't rid myself of it. Maybe the fault lies in me. She certainly got rid of it before the night was over. I locked it away in the safe myself."

"Which seems to suggest Rebecca might have been another one of Dad's victims. He set her up? Maybe marked her in everyone's eyes?" Ally suggested shrewdly.

"Talk to her and find out," Brod said.

"You sound like the answer is important to you." Ally's mind was working overtime. She wondered about this Rebecca Hunt who had made such an impression not only on her father but on Brod as well.

"It's easy to see she'd get to a man, Ally," Brod confirmed what she was thinking. "The thing is I can't reconcile all my images of her."

To his sister the look in Brod's eyes could only be described as tormented.

The four of them sat at one end of the long mahogany dinner table, eating without appetite, the conversation muted and desultory. Even Fee, a genuine extrovert, was subdued by the tragedy that had overtaken them. Given what she had heard, Ally didn't know what to expect when she finally met Rebecca Hunt. Rebecca had not intruded on her homecoming but had insisted on waiting until dinner to be introduced.

Now Ally watched the other younger woman as she sat quietly beside Fee. Just as Brod had said she was simply beautiful, Ally thought. Dressed in a deep violet shift dress that lightly skimmed her figure. The light from the chandelier glossed her smooth dark hair and illuminated the creamy white skin. She was small, inches shorter than Ally who was five-seven but she carried herself so elegantly she appeared taller. Her eyes, Ally considered, were her most striking feature apart from the piquancy of that full mouth. Every time she lifted her head, they glittered like diamonds with the light on them. She had a good hand shake, a lovely voice, and a decidedly refined air. She wasn't overly friendly, which Ally didn't expect at this time but when she did speak she said all the right things.

Ally couldn't fault her. In truth she didn't want to fault her at all. Rebecca Hunt didn't strike her as an opportunist or a social climber though Ally could well see how her father had become infatuated. Rather she struck Ally as a young professional woman like herself, who was very good at what she did, but hiding a multitude of hurts behind a carefully constructed facade. Ally's own dysfunctional childhood and adolescence gave her an insight into such things.

During the course of the evening Ally noticed, too, the tensions that were running back and forth between Rebecca and her brother, the intensity of the glances as though each was speaking to the other with their eyes. The tension peaked around half past nine when Rebecca rose gracefully to her feet.

"I must leave you all to speak privately," she said with the most exquisite sad smile. "I know you must want to." She addressed Ally directly. "I'm so glad to have finally met you, Ally. I've heard so many lovely things about you. Now I'll enjoy your show even more when I watch it. Night, Fee. You've been so kind asking me to stay on but I really feel I should return to Sydney after—'' she faltered briefly ''—the funeral. There will be lots of planes flying in and out. I'm sure I could arrange a lift to some point.''

"How about the Never Never," Brod said discordially looking at her hard. "I thought we'd discussed this, Rebecca."

"Well we did." She looked flustered. "But Francesca will be arriving. Ally is staying on. You don't need me. We can leave the biography, Fee, until such time as you're ready to start again." The very tautness of her face showed her anguish.

"But, darling, I don't want that at all," Fee protested, casting aside her wondrously beautiful deeply fringed silk shawl. "I don't want you to live with this…sadness on your own. You've sustained a bad shock. Our lives have become entwined. Besides I'm looking on working on the biography as a sort of cure. A healing if you will. We haven't spoken one real word about my childhood yet. Stewart was alive and things were…'' She threw up her hands theatrically.

"God, Fee, you're not going to make a full confession now he's gone?" Brod asked with a wry groan.

"What's wrong with the truth?" Fee demanded. "You don't know how miserable Stewart made me when we were children. He was a devil of a liar. Got me into terrible trouble all the time. Said I did everything.''

"You probably did," Ally observed with the same wry affection Brod used when he spoke to his aunt. Ally transferred her gaze to Rebecca. "Please don't think of going on account of me, Rebecca. I can see we'll get on fine. Fran is a lovely person. Fee and I both want you to meet her. Anyway you heard Fee. She means to go on with the book.''

Rebecca looked touched, but adamant. ''You're being so nice but I really think…''

''Rebecca, why don't I walk you up to your room,'' Brod intervened, rising to his impressive height. ''I can plead with you on the way.''

''Do that, Brod,'' Fee said in heartfelt tones. ''Rebecca really doesn't have anyone to go to. She told me. This isn't a kindness, Rebecca. We really want you.'' She sounded very definite as indeed she was.

''What's with Rebecca and Brod?'' Ally asked her aunt in a fraught undertone as soon as the two had left the room. ''You don't need an antennae to pick up the vibes.''

''To be honest, darling, I think Brod's fighting his attraction to her. I think he's going through a bit of hell over your father, and Stewart's claim Rebecca knew all about Cecilia's Necklace before she wore it.''

Ally continued to stare at her aunt. ''You don't believe that?''

''Darling, I don't want to say it, but I know what a liar your dear father was.''

''Well he's at rest now,'' Ally sighed.

''Wouldn't it be horrible if he weren't,'' said Fee.

Both of them waited until they were in the upper hallway before either of them spoke.

Even then in mounting furious undertones. ''What a little coward you are waiting until you had Fee and Ally for cover,'' Brod accused her, when he really wanted to touch her. Soothe her.

''Am I going to go to hell for it?'' Rebecca's pale

face flushed with anger. "Why do you want me here, Brod? To mete out further punishment?"

His lean face tautened. "No such thing has occurred to me. Besides it seems to me you're punishing yourself. How's it going to help you to run off?"

Rebecca let out a long mournful sigh. "Damn it, I'm not running off. I just don't want to intrude."

He couldn't help himself. He exploded. "Hell, that's good. You turn the whole household upside down, me included, now you're talking about hitching a ride on the first plane out of here. It doesn't fit the pattern."

"I thought it was what you wanted?" She stared up into his face, afraid of his power, his magnetism. She didn't need this upheaval in her ordered life.

He actually groaned. "I don't know what I want with your face distracting me. Maybe you ought to think of Fee. She employed you to do a job. You're a professional aren't you? It must have sunk in she wants you here." He gave a quiet, ironic laugh. "You've even talked Ally around."

Rebecca took a few rapid little steps away from him and went no further. "Honestly you take my breath away. I can't believe Ally's your sister."

"Good Lord, you haven't noticed we're very much alike?"

"Ally is a beautiful person." Rebecca ignored the mockery. "You're decidedly not. If I were you I'd be ashamed."

He tossed the idea around for a moment. "Tell me what I'm supposed to be ashamed of and I'll work on it," he said. Then suddenly in a voice that moved her powerfully he added, "I want you to stay, Rebecca."

Her heart quite literally rocked. "You want to keep an eye on me?" Despite herself her voice trembled.

"Like inches away." He moved closer, as graceful and soundless as a panther.

"I don't want trouble, Brod." She raised her chin.

"That doesn't seem to matter when it obviously comes after you. What are you afraid of, Rebecca?"

"I might ask the same question of you?"

He reached out and drew a shivery finger down her cheek. "As it turns out I don't have the answer. What I particularly need to hear is more about you. You already know a lot about me. I think it's time you started talking. You don't speak of family. Of friends, lovers."

"I don't choose to," Rebecca said, the perverse pleasure in his company so keen she couldn't move.

"Fee said you had no one to go back to. What did she mean?"

She ought to try to move. *Now.* Yet her body turned more fully towards him like a flower to the sun. "My mother died when I was fourteen," she began quietly even now feeling the terrible pain of severance. "She survived a car accident but complications from her injuries killed her a few years later. My father remarried. I see him and his other family as much as I can but he lives in Hong Kong. He was an airline pilot. The best. He's retired now." She touched the tip of her tongue to her suddenly dry lips.

"Don't do that," he said in a slow deep voice.

"Brod, I can't stay here in this house. This beautiful sad house."

"Why do you think that is? Come on, tell me." He swooped to take hold of her wrists, drawing her close against him, bending his dark head to kiss her a little roughly but so sweetly, so passionately on her mouth.

He was becoming so precious to her she was really afraid. Don't stop. Don't ever stop. The feeling was stupendous. Her heart was burning inside her like a flame.

But he did, lifting his head like a man who was spell-bound.

"This thing between us, I don't want to hurt you," he muttered, not even sure if he believed it himself.

"But it scares me." There she'd admitted it.

"You're the one with the powers." Now there was a shimmer of male hostility. "These past few days have been hell."

She recognised that herself. "I never thought for a moment your father—" She broke off, too upset to go on.

"Would fall in love with you. Want to marry you?" He held her away from him so he could stare down into her face.

"No." She averted her head so he could only see the curve of her cheek.

Something flickered in his brilliant eyes. How to control this power she had. "I don't see we're getting any-where discussing this." He removed his hands quietly, watching her brush a long strand of her hair away from her face. "Don't embarrass us by calling on anyone to give you a lift, Rebecca," he said. "Don't hurt Fee's feelings. When you're ready to tell me what lies under that porcelain exterior, I'm here."

How can I tell him, Rebecca thought, her eyes trained on his tall figure until he reached the central staircase and without a backwards glance disappeared down the steps. Back to his family.

I had a family, too, Rebecca thought, walking deso-lately to her room, closing the door. A very happy fam-ily until her mother, a passenger in a friend's car, was badly injured when the car they were travelling in was struck by a speeding vehicle. Her mother's friend was killed. Her mother spent the rest of her life in a wheelchair devotedly nursed by her husband and daughter. A few years after her mother's premature death, her father remarried. A beautiful Eurasian women he met in Hong Kong. At this time she was at boarding school while her father shuttled between Hong Kong and Sydney. Even so they remained close and Vivienne, her stepmother, never let a birthday go past without sending some wonderful present. Vacations were spent in all sorts of exotic places. Bangkok, Phuket, Bali, twice to Marrekesch, but things settled down after Vivienne had her first child, an adorable little boy they called Jean Phillipe. A little girl, Christina, followed two years later.

It was at university she met Martyn. He was a few years older, studying law. She was doing an arts degree majoring in journalism. Although she was making lots of friends she and Martyn soon became a pair. He was exceptionally bright, good-looking, of excellent family, an only child. If Rebecca was soon to find his mother was very possessive she kept it to herself. Anyway Meredith actually approved of her if a little unhappy about the fact Rebecca's father had married a Eurasian who could have run rings around Meredith in any direction.

They were married when she was twenty and Martyn twenty-four. At first they'd been happy only Martyn didn't think she had any real need to finish her studies. His family were well-off. He was an up-and-coming young lawyer with a prestigious firm who had selected him because of his brilliant results. His mother had never worked. She had dedicated her life to becoming the perfect wife and mother. That was Meredith's primary responsibility in life. She fussed endlessly over her husband and son, kept a splendid house for them, arranged all the frequent entertaining. Rebecca's goal should be the same. It was supposed to be an all encompassing role. And some years on—Martyn was in no hurry to start a family—they would have children. Two only. A boy and a girl.

It took Rebecca a while to realise Martyn didn't want friends. Or her friends at least. He didn't want to invite them around to their very comfortable town house, a wedding present from his parents, he didn't want to go to any of their parties. Gradually people stopped asking altogether. As one of her girlfriends told her: "Martyn only wants you for himself, Becky. You're supposed to be so smart. Can't you see that?"

The marriage had lasted exactly three years. No time. An eternity. She refused point-blank to give up her studies. Her generation wanted a fulfilling job. She was supposed to be an outstanding student. At which point Martyn had always thrown back his head and laughed. "Journalism? What the heck's that? Stay at home and write a bestseller."

The arguments began. She felt he was caging her. Destroying her friendships. It wasn't a life, just the two of them all the time. It dawned on her that Martyn, for all his legal brain, wasn't interesting enough. What was important to him was he had her undivided attention.

The physical abuse started in the last year. First a hard slap across the face that sent her flying. Of course she had reacted in horror. Her father had been so gentle towards her and her mother. She left their town house that very night staying with Kim her most faithful friend. Martyn had come after her, in tears, begging her forgiveness.

"Don't go, Becky," Kim warned her. "It will only start again."

But he was her husband. She'd taken her marriage vows very seriously. The last time he hit her she ended in hospital with cracked ribs.

The marriage was over. She had her life back. Though it wasn't that simple. She had to endure a period of terrible harassment until she threatened to go to the head of his law firm, a fine man who liked her, to lodge a complaint. Soon after she moved away to London, determined nothing like that would ever happen to her again. It had been a long time before she had entered into another relationship. But somehow no one had ever touched her heart.

Until now.

CHAPTER SIX

AROUND them, everywhere they looked the ancient plains stretched to the horizon, the needle leaved clumps of spinifex that dotted them bleached bright gold against the fiery red of the sand they stabilised. Above them arched the limitless peacock-blue sky that at three o'clock in the afternoon was ruled by a scorching sun. People had come from all over the Outback to the vast station, this vast emptiness, to attend Stewart Kinross's funeral. Almost everybody except the infirm or the elderly had trudged to the low ridge where the Kinross family since the time of settlement had buried their dead.

The family cemetery in itself was impressive, surrounded by a stone wall with elaborate black wrought iron gates. Small and immense headstones were erected inside, some side by side. Kinross men and women. Children. Rebecca's eyes blurred as she tried to read some of the poignant legends on the marbles, unutterably saddened to see babies had died.

No tears from the family. Brod stood his six foot three, his hands clasped before him, his handsome blue-black head bowed. Ally dressed from head to toe in black stood with Fee, similarly attired as was Fee's lovely daughter, Francesca, the sheer perfection of her English skin and her marvellous titian hair a striking foil to her black dress relieved only by an obviously valuable string of pearls.

Other members of the extended family crowded

around, friends, VIP's, businessmen, partners in many of the Kinross ventures. Prominent not only by virtue of their height and physical presence, were the Cameron brothers, Rafe and Grant, their unprotected bare heads with the fabulous glint of gold.

Rebecca in a dark grey wide-brimmed straw hat Ally had lent her, which matched the only suitable dress she had with her, a discreet charcoal-grey, was glad of the sunglasses that hid her eyes.

The clergyman, well-known to the family, continued with the service while Rebecca gripped her fingers waiting for it all to end. She half turned away at the final moments when the heavy ornate casket was lowered into the ground, unable to witness it. Her own mother's funeral came back to her with dreadful clarity. She and her father had stood rigid, fighting to keep back the floodgates but at that point they had both succumbed to unrestrained weeping. At least her father had found happiness as her mother would have wanted.

That hadn't been her lot. Martyn had treated her so badly but in the end she had been far from powerless. She had reclaimed her life. Known success, won the respect of her peers. She'd had no way of knowing when she accepted Fiona Kinross's commission to write her biography such high drama would be unleashed. What was she doing here on this day of all days? How had she ever become so deeply involved with the Kinross family, not knowing at that point Stewart Kinross had carefully planned it all.

To Rebecca it didn't seem possible Stewart was dead. Only she and Brod had seen him die. Nothing had prepared her for such a shock.

Back at the homestead, people milled through the main reception rooms and out onto the surrounding verandahs, partaking of the food and drink that had been prepared for them. Most stuck to tea and coffee with the selection of sandwiches but some of the men were knocking back whisky like it was mineral water. The conversation, though subdued, created such a persistent buzz it drove Ally, her nerves much on edge, to the far end of the side verandah. Worse yet to come. At some point she had to face Rafe. The very last thing she needed was hundreds of eyes on them.

Like most of the other women she had taken off her hat. Now damp tendrils of her curly hair that she had worn in a thick upturned roll at the back clung to her temples and nape. She turned away to look out over an avenue of palms. The home gardens were ablaze with colour. Soon the desert would burst into flower. Give it a month. The big storm that had robbed her father of his life would bring to Kimbara a marvellous profusion of wildflowers, millions and millions of everlastings, papery pink, bright yellow and white. When she was a little girl she had rejoiced in the way the everlastings didn't wilt. The Sturt Peas, named after the explorer, would trail their long stems of crimson flowers across the mulga plains, the fleshy leaved parakeelyas forming radiating patterns in the sand. The incredibly tough spinifex would turn from sun-scorched gold to deep green then later when it sent up its seed bearing stems great tracts of spinifex country were transformed from desert to a landscape that almost resembled vast fields of wheat.

How she missed it all! Though she had become successful at what she did—had indeed inherited some of her aunt Fee's great talent—she never felt truly at home in the city. This was her world, this incredible living desert; this sun-scorched land of fiery colours. The lush seaboard had its own unique beauty, marvellous Sydney Harbour, but nothing spoke to her like her own fascinating home, Kimbara. Brod's now. Lost in her thoughts, Ally started visibly when a man addressed her.

"Ally?"

She turned away from the white wrought-iron balustrade to find Rafe studying her out of half-hooded gold-flecked hazel eyes. She willed on herself calmness but her head had gone spinning. A big man, even with her wearing her black high heeled shoes, she had to look up at him. His attitude was courteous. Rafe was always the gentleman, but a remoteness was there in his narrowed gaze. In the heat of the afternoon like most of the men he had taken off his jacket, his crisp white shirt showing the breadth of his shoulders, the top button of his collar undone so he could loosen his black tie. He looked as stunning as ever, the straight chiselled nose, the squarish chin with its distinctive cleft, the wide mouth, the clear gold skin that was so arresting with his thick shock of gold hair.

"Well am I looking better or worse?" he broke into her examination, his deep voice faintly wry.

"You look great, Rafe," she said. A masterly understatement. Like Brod he had found an impressive maturity.

"I haven't had a chance to tell you how shocked we were, Grant and I, by Stewart's death," he said with formal sincerity. "Please accept my condolences. Grant will catch up with you. He's still paying his respects to the rest of the family."

"Thank you, Rafe," she murmured, her emotions intensifying by the second.

"You're too thin," he said abruptly when he hadn't intended to say it at all.

"Have to be," she answered flippantly to cover her own agitation at seeing him. "The camera adds pounds."

Again he allowed his eyes to move over her. "You look like the breeze might blow you over," he said finally, dismayed by the stirring in his blood. "So, your career? Is it going as planned? You seem to have hit the jackpot with your show. Top of the ratings."

She leaned back against the railing. "It is a lot of hard work. I go straight home when the shooting is over. I have to learn my lines. I have to be up very early in the morning."

"That shouldn't leave you looking so stressed out," he said, disturbed despite himself at her look of strain.

"Is that how I seem?"

"Even given the shock of your father's death, you've altered." He wasn't going to tell her she looked beautiful, if too fragile for her height. The Ally he had held in his arms had more cover on those long classy bones. More curve to her warm, sweet breasts. How marvellous it had been then. Fantastic when they were alone together. Ally, his heart's desire. On the very day he intended to ask her to marry him, she provoked a blazing argument that left him dazed....

"I want it all to stop for a while, Rafe," she had cried, the tears smudging her cheeks, dust streaked from their ride, her long thick lashes stuck together spikily. "I want my own space!" When he finally calmed her down she claimed she loved him too much. That made him laugh. Not for long. Ally of the dark brown hair and slanting green eyes had made a fool of him with a capital *F*. She had run away to Sydney leaving him bereft. His heart broken until he picked himself up determined never to believe a woman again.

And what was he supposed to say to her now she was back? If only for her father's funeral. He knew, couldn't help knowing, he could have just about any woman he wanted. He'd had his casual affairs. He had to take it for granted Ally had had hers. She had it all. Beauty, freedom, style, wealth, a career that put her face on the cover of glossy magazines. God help him he had even bought a few. For what purpose? Another man might have thrown darts at her image. The great thing was he was over her. The Ally he had loved never really existed.

"You look so serious, Rafe," she was saying, lifting her emerald-green eyes to him. "Even grim. What could you possibly be thinking about?"

"I don't think you'd want to know," he said.

She couldn't bear the look in his eyes. "Not if it's about me. I know you despise me."

He heard his own deep-throated laugh. "Ally, beautiful as you are, it might be as well for you to know I'm now indifferent to your many charms. Fact is you're not the girl I knew all my life."

"You've written me off?" She stayed very still.

He nodded. "Had to." When he would have moved heaven and earth for her. "What about you? Anyone important in your life?"

She pushed tendrils of hair from her aching forehead. "People come and go, Rafe," she said, careful not to look at him. Not a one of them could measure up to you.

"How long are you staying?" He, too, sounded careful.

"A week. That's all I can spare. It's wonderful to be home. The comfort of it."

"Even if you were driven back by your father's death?"

She lifted her beautiful sad eyes. "You know all about our family, Rafe. You know why I'm not crying though I'm in mourning for what might have been. Like Brod. Dad never cared for me, Rafe. Think of that! He broke my heart."

He fought against saying it. Lost. "There's evidence you've got one?" One step. One error and he would pull her into his arms.

"I loved you. You were my world." With so many onlookers she managed to keep her face composed though her voice was unsteady.

"But you couldn't rest until you tried something else?"

"If only that were all of it!" she exclaimed. "I was too young, Rafe. I couldn't handle what we had. Our relationship was so powerful."

"Is that how you analyse it?" He spoke as though it were a clinical question.

"For what it's worth!" She managed to nod at people who were looking their way. Amanda Someone was staring. She seemed jealous.

"Well it doesn't matter now," said Rafe.

Grant followed Francesca's slender, black-clad figure out into the corridor. "How's the jet lag?" he asked, real concern on his open, strong-boned face.

"I made a fool of myself didn't I?"

He looked down at her and smiled. "I'd probably have fainted myself after such a long, gruelling trip."

She was amused by the very idea. He exuded such

strength. "At least you were there to catch me." Within moments of walking into the bush terminal she, who prided herself on being a good traveller, had crumpled like a doll.

"I had the feeling I was catching a flower." He held her with his eyes gazing into what he considered the prettiest face he had ever seen. He knew Ally, the Kinross who had broken his brother's heart was beautiful in her vibrant challenging way. The young woman who had come to write Fee's biography, Rebecca, was beautiful as well, but so cool and controlled she might have been carved out of ice. This lovely creature had a warmth, a *sweetness,* a kind of innocence written all over her. It affected him powerfully.

"Don't write me off, Grant," she teased him gently. "There's a lot more to me than you can see."

"Was I doing that?" One tawny eyebrow shot up comically. "Writing you off?"

She nodded her head, all the while smiling at him. "I can see you don't think I'd fit in here."

Show me a rose growing in the desert, he thought. She was soft voiced. A lovely voice. Cut-glass accent but natural. She put him irresistibly in mind of a rose. Pink rose in a sterling-silver bud vase. "I do have that feeling, yes," he admitted. "For one thing you wouldn't be used to the heat." Yet he couldn't see the tiniest bead of perspiration on her flawless skin.

Francesca could have hooted. "You're not going to believe this but I think the heat's fantastic. I left some very miserable cold and wet weather at home. I want to thank you again, Grant, for coming to my rescue. For flying me in. I know you're a busy man."

That he was. "There aren't enough hours in the day. I've got plans. Big plans. I want to—" He broke off and shot her a wry look. "I'm sorry. You didn't come all the way to hear Grant Cameron's visions."

"No, tell me." She took his arm. Beautiful, gentle, soft. "I know you run the helicopter service, of course. But you want to start your own airline to service the Inland. Is that right? Passengers and freight?"

He gave her a surprised, interrogating look. "Who told you that?" An elderly couple moved out into the corridor so Grant took Francesca's elbow moving her further down the parqueted passageway towards a side verandah.

"It was Brod." Francesca stopped walking to look up at him, struck again by his rare tawny colouring, the depth of copper in the thick burnt-gold hair swept off his wide forehead, the gleaming near-topaz eyes. "Brod is tremendously interested in your schemes. So am I."

He saw the sincerity. Was warmed by it. "That's wonderful." He grinned. "But are you sure you've got the time? I thought you were going home to your glamorous life in little more than a week?"

The topaz eyes were twinkling but Francesca knew what he was thinking. "I have to tell you, Grant Cameron, I'm finding it a lot more glamorous here."

Where else could you find a grand mansion in the frightening isolation and extraordinary savage beauty of the Australian desert? Where else could you find such a magnificent man? She might be setting herself up for a little heartache, a brief romance with no hope of resolution, but one thing was certain—Grant Cameron drew her like a flame.

Long after the household had retired, all of them diminished by the events of the day, Rebecca, more shocked than she knew, sought medication for a headache worse than anything she had experienced for a long time. Perhaps she was running a high fever. She seemed very hot. She stumbled into the adjoining bathroom to see if there were any aspirin left.

One. No good. She was going to need more painkiller. It was downstairs in the large first-aid room stocked like a pharmacy. Her mind was whirling from her compulsive reviewing of the day. She couldn't forget Stewart Kinross's last words to her.

"There's no way I'll let him have you."

She couldn't possibly tell Brod that. It would drive him crazy.

She remembered the way she urged the mare Jeeba away. Poor Jeeba! It upset her terribly the mare had to be destroyed. Horses with their delicate legs. She didn't want to think about it but loving horses so much she couldn't push it away. Although the women of the family, Fee, Ally, and Francesca had supported her fully throughout the long afternoon, Brod hadn't come within ten feet of her. Of course people never stopped coming up to him, keeping him contained until it was all over but he had kept his distance from her as though she were poison she thought bleakly.

And there was still something he didn't know. He didn't know she had once been married. He didn't know that marriage had ended disastrously. Shattered beyond repair. He had invited her to talk to him but she had built up so many defences she doubted if she could speak of that awful time.

Dear God, she didn't want to be reminded. She didn't want to be reminded of the dreadful mistake she had made. The number of times she had cried. The shame of the things Martyn had done. She certainly didn't want to be reminded of Martyn's mother's visit.

Meredith had accused her—if Rebecca hadn't caused her injuries herself!—of driving him to hurting his wife with her demands for freedom, for a career. She had reneged on her sacred marriage vows. Back and forth they went, she losing the argument in the light of her mother-in-law's unswerving belief in her son, the fineness of his character.

Meredith had pleaded with her to go back to Martyn. He loved her. Didn't she know that? He would give her whatever she wanted if only she would go back.

Anything was better than going back. She was certain Meredith would face this problem again. Martyn liked making women suffer. Perhaps he was getting square with a suffocatingly possessive mother.

How could she tell Brod all about that? Though God knows it couldn't have been easy for him and Ally growing up in this house. Even Fee had spoken about her brother's destructive qualities. Now Rebecca began to see Lucille Kinross, like her, had been forced to flee a desperately unhappy marriage.

With a little shake of her pounding head, Rebecca caught up her robe, tying the sash tightly around her waist. There was no hope for her. She would live with her guilts forever. Real or imagined. She had never given Stewart Kinross the slightest encouragement. Indeed the thought had never entered her head but perhaps she had overresponded to his many kindnesses to her? She cursed some quality in her that drew certain men to her.

Downstairs she thought she heard a sound. She stood perfectly still for a moment trying to trace breathing, soft footsteps, anything. Both floors of the huge house were dimly lit with wall sconces, brighter at the head of the central staircase so no one could miss their footing if they descended during the night. She was conscious her heart was beating fast within her.

No one at all. Just all the little sounds of a darkened old house.

She had come downstairs for a purpose. Now she almost flew down the corridor that led to the kitchen taking a right turn to the large, well-stocked first-aid room. Lots of accidents, big and small went on at Outback stations. Kimbara was always prepared. When she snapped on the switch the light almost blinded her so brilliantly did it bounce off the white walls and fittings. She saw her own startled face in a mirrored cabinet. She might have been a ghost her skin was so pale but her floating black hair was very real, the sleeplessness was in her shadowed gaze.

She needed something to work a miracle. She walked to one of the cabinets she knew housed a range of painkillers, letting her eyes run along the packages.

"I didn't think I dreamed it," a dark, eloquent voice said behind her.

"Brod!" She swung around, in her agitation dropping a packet to the black-and-white tiled floor. Now colour whipped into her skin as though a switch had been thrown.

"What's the matter?" He bent to retrieve the package, turning it over in his hand. "A headache?"

She lifted her hand to her temple. "I don't think I've had such a bad one in my life." Take that back, she thought dismally. In the last few years.

"Maybe these won't be strong enough." A frown drew his black brows together.

"I'll try them anyway."

"Why are you whispering?" He walked to another cupboard, took out a clean glass and filled it at the sink.

"Because it's very late. Because you frightened me." She gave a husky laugh. "What the heck else do I need?"

"Don't let's get into an argument." He turned to her, his eyes moving over her. "You look very pale. The fact is, Rebecca, I know how you feel. Only I've been drowning my pain with a few shots of whisky."

He pushed two tablets from their silvered sockets into the palm of his hand. "Here," he said quietly. "I hope they do some good."

She took them from him, feeling the rough calluses on his palms, wondering for a rocky moment how those same hands would feel on her body. She choked a little as the tablets seemed to stick in her upper chest, but swallowed more water at his urging.

"Come and talk to me," he said in a deep, low voice. "I'll let you lie quietly. I don't want to be alone."

Neither did she, still she hesitated. "Maybe..."

"Maybe what?" He looked down at her, so small in her slippered feet, her silky robe like the pale green sheaf of a flower.

"Maybe it's not a good idea, Brod."

"I can't think of one better." He took her hand, his handsome face taut and angular, his magnificent body in his everyday jeans, his soft blue shirt near undone to the waist in the sultry heat.

"Where are we going?" she asked, captured by his touch.

"Don't panic. I'm not taking you up to bed."

God, in her confusion she nearly cried out. Take me. Take me. *Hold me.* I want to be lost. Instead she walked with him very quietly. They paused at the study and he reached around with his hand to find the light switch. "You can lie down on the sofa," he told her, releasing her hand. ''You don't have to talk if you don't want to I just need you to be there.''

She went to the big burgundy chesterfield and curled into it, drawing up her feet. He picked up a cushion from an armchair and tucked it behind her head. ''Relax, Rebecca. There's nothing to dread. I wouldn't hurt you for the world.''

A soft cry of protest came out of her. ''I never thought you would.'' The last thing she feared from him was sexual harassment. What she feared was her own passion, the tumultuous spill of emotion. She lay back and he ran his hand briefly through her hair.

''What a terrible day.''

''I know. My heart aches for you, Brod.''

He gave a short groan. ''I'm finding it very difficult to mourn my father, Rebecca. Does that sound terrible? The hell is I'm not ashamed of it, either.'' He moved back across the room and sat in a big deep armchair with his grandfather's gaze on him. ''Close your eyes,'' he advised. ''Let the pain killers work.

''Parents shouldn't kill their children's love, Rebecca. Children have a right to love. Otherwise why bring them into the world?

''Dad chose an *heir*,'' Brod continued in a pained voice. ''Kimbara needs heirs. He always acted as though I was one hell of a disappointment to him. Ally, too. Can you believe it? My beautiful, gifted sister. My mother was a hell of a disappointment to him, too. She couldn't live with that. She ran off.''

Was it time to say something about her own marriage.

The time passed.

''Sometimes I think this house has a curse on it,'' Brod sighed. ''The first Kinross bride, Cecilia, married the wrong man and was forced to live with it. She should have been a Cameron. My mother was another matter. After she was killed my father called me into this very study and told me all about it.

"No one gets away from me," he said.

Rebecca's eyes swept open. "He said that to his own child?"

Brod nodded. "He wasn't a man to pull punches. In our ignorance and pain Ally and I thought our mother had deserted us. The one parent who loved us. Later we knew what it was all about. You wouldn't have fared well with my father, Rebecca."

"Trust me," Rebecca pleaded, knowing full well it would take time.

"Well it doesn't matter any more." He released another sigh. "Has your headache eased?"

"A little."

"Let's see if this works." He came behind her and began to stroke her temples, his fingers moving with exquisite gentleness.

He had to be a magician. Almost at once she felt a warmth through her body, a warmth that spread to the smooth area under his healing hands.

"Oh, that's good. You have magic in your hands." She released a fluttery breath, loving what he was doing.

"Keep your eyes closed." His fingers began to move over her forehead and cheeks. They traced the curve of her eyebrows, the closed lids of her eyes, the whorls of her ears back to her satin temples as if he had all the time in the world. "Better?" he asked after a long while.

"Oh, yes!" she said softly, desiring his touch.

Then he picked her up. Cradling her before he low-

ered himself onto the chesterfield with her in his arms.
"I just want to hold you. Okay?"

She let her head fall back against his shoulder. "I
want to know all about you," she whispered. "Tell
me."

For a moment he buried his face in her fragrant hair,
then he began to speak, almost to himself at first. "It
was really my grandfather who reared us. He was a
wonderful man. Some people are kind enough to say
I'm like him. He taught Ally and me to believe in our-
selves…"

"Go on." She settled herself more comfortably and
his arms closed around her. Her headache, miraculously,
was gone. She was where she wanted to be.

When he finished speaking she knew more about his
life than possibly anyone in the world, including his
sister.

Somehow her position had changed. Her head was
now pressed into his chest. One of her hands was
clutching his shirt and she was breathing in his warm
masculinity like incense.

"You're a good listener," he only half joked, wondering how so slight a body could seem so soft and
voluptuous. God, if only…if only…

She lifted her head and stared into his eyes. "I didn't
want you to stop."

"But I want to know who *you* are." He wound his
hand through her long hair, moving very quietly into
kissing her, wanting to do nothing against her will but
moving perilously close to a man's driving hunger.
"Rebecca?" he murmured against the side of her
mouth.

She couldn't help herself. Her arm slid up around his

neck arousing him still further. She clung to him, her body twisting in yearning.

His hands moved down over her breasts, caressing them through the thin silky covering of her clothes, his thumbs gathering the tender nipples into tight electric buds. The sweet feverishness of it. He had fallen madly in love with her without realising it. This beautiful mysterious creature. All at once he needed to touch her naked flesh. He thrust his hand inside her gown as she turned her head into his throat.

"We're mad to do this," she whispered even as she let him touch her so intimately.

"When there's not the tiniest part of you I don't hunger for?"

"Someone might come." Yet she put her arms around him and held him to her breast.

"I don't know that they'll get through that locked door," he answered softly, his hands moving up and down the curve of her back, drawing her ever closer. This was the day of his father's funeral yet he was doing the strangest thing. Making love to Rebecca. Losing himself in her and her great fascination. Her mouth was her most revealing feature. It identified the deep well of passion that was in her. He looked down at her satiny dark hair tumbled over her eyes.

"Spend the night with me," he urged, his voice a little harsh with arousal.

She closed her eyes against his plea. "Then nothing will be the same again."

"Nothing has been the same since the moment I laid eyes on you," he mocked. The luminous eyes. The passionate mouth. Oh, yes, the mouth.

He kissed it again, so deeply she shuddered. "I want you beside me when I wake up."

"I can't do this." But her heart was racing, her whole body shot through with desire.

"You don't have a husband to betray?" he reminded her, exulting in her body's response to him. "Isn't that right?" He stared directly into her eyes, his own breathtakingly blue.

"No husband," she said at last.

"Then you need a man to tell you how beautiful you are?" He lifted her, thinking he could use the small spiralling staircase at the end of the hall. There was no turning back now. His need for her was too immense.

CHAPTER SEVEN

ONCE Ally and Francesca went home after a stay that meant a great deal to all of them, Rebecca and Fee settled into a definite routine. They worked steadily on Fee's biography, averaging four or five hours each day but this time Rebecca began to delve more deeply into Fee's colourful life, looking for more information and treasures. This wasn't going to be a book that let *all* the family skeletons out of the closet but after that special night with Brod who had talked so eloquently and movingly about his life, Rebecca found she wanted to draw much more out of Fee than the glossed up and glossed over versions Fee had presented her thus far. Now thanks to Brod, Rebecca felt she had a far greater insight into the family; but there were difficulties.

"Darling, do you think we should say that?" Fee often asked doubtfully when in the course of their discussions Fee came up with some revelation.

Rebecca invariably replied; "Do we want an extraordinary memoir, Fee, a first-rate biography, or a giveaway book for the coffee table?"

Fee being an extraordinary person wanted an extraordinary memoir so they restarted their journey going beyond Fee's childhood on Kimbara, the only daughter of the legendary cattle king, Sir Andrew Kinross and Constance McQuillan Kinross, a renowned horsewoman, herself the only daughter of a great pastoral family who had died a premature death at the age of forty-two after being tragically thrown from her horse in a cross-country race.

"I want it to be more than a biography of your life, Fee," Rebecca told her. "I'd like you to reflect upon *family*. A prominent landed family. A complex family as far as I can see. Marriages, starting with Ewan Kinross and Cecilia. Family influences. This business of inheritance, relationships."

"Lord, darling, you're looking at the best part of 150 years," Fee answered wryly. "That's a long time in this part of the world."

"It's more an overview of the family history I want, Fee. When you're speaking you paint such vivid word pictures. Brod has the same ability. Ally has it, too. I want to get it into print. Ally told me so much during her stay. It was wonderful to be able to speak together so freely. Brod even more. I'd like to use their recollections as well. I see this book as a marvellous kaleidoscope of Outback life as lived by a family who pioneered this vast area."

Fee smiled at Rebecca's youthful enthusiasm. "Heavens, darling, some of the stories would make anyone flinch."

"All your stories are safe with me, Fee," Rebecca told her seriously. "In the end we'll only reveal as much as you want to. I'm sure the reader will appreciate your candour, your generosity of spirit, not to mention your wicked sense of humour."

"If we're talking wicked I suppose I have to mention my sex life," Fee said in her rich, deep voice.

"Well it's not exactly a mystery, Fee," Rebecca teased. "We can change names of individuals to protect their privacy."

Fee looked saddened. "Darling, most of them are

dead now, including my poor brother. I've found the most marvellous old photographs of him and me. We can use them. A lot of Lucille somebody has obviously hidden.''

''That was Brod,'' Rebecca openly admitted, seeing Lucille's lovely face in her mind.

''Good God!'' Fee gave a great sigh. ''His father would have been furious had he known.'' The green eyes were searching. ''For that matter, darling, how did you know? Brod has never mentioned hiding the photographs to me?''

Rebecca met Fee's gaze calmly. ''We had a long conversation one night.''

Fee lowered her head, knowing full well there was something going on between Rebecca and Brod. ''Why not?'' she replied. ''I'm glad. You and Brod seem to be in harmony these days.'' She was far from oblivious to this new dimension in their relationship. ''Both Brod and Ally have had to keep far too much to themselves,'' she added. ''Now, let's have a cup of tea, then we'll get right down to it. This biography is taking on an entirely new character.''

''Thank Brod,'' Rebecca suggested. No matter what happened she would always remember she'd had this very special time with him.

Brod came in around noon, telling them with wry humour about a staff dispute he had to settle. He snatched a few sandwiches and coffee, which he ate in Fee's sitting room, listening to Fee unearth another piece of family archaeology he had some doubts she ought to mention.

''Hell, Fee, you're going to reveal all our secrets,''

he ventured, tossing the last sandwich aside.

"Within limits, darling," Fee corrected. "Silence won't sell the book. Besides Rebecca wants me to make the book more powerful."

"Then we might get Rebecca to write one of her own." His blue eyes flashed provocatively towards Rebecca's face. "From what you say, it's far from portraying some members of our family in a good light. Ewan who seemed to have tricked Cecilia into marrying him. Alistair who ran off to Paris supposedly to paint but ran through a fortune instead. Great Aunt Eloise who married a thirty-five-year-old man when she was sixty years old."

"But, darling, she was beautiful. She was famous," Fee offered by way of explanation, turning her head to preen in a gilt-framed mirror. "She was also an heiress," Brod said, rising to his feet and adjusting the red bandanna around his tanned neck, "and her husband didn't have a razoo." He brought his brilliant glance to rest on Rebecca. "If Fee can spare you for an hour or so later on this afternoon, I'd like to take you out and show you the wildflowers. I promised you they'd put on a tremendous display after all the heavy showers. Would you like to come, too, Fee?"

"Not today, darling," Fee answered casually, not about to play gooseberry. "I have a lot of mail to catch up on. That invitation to direct the Milton Theatre Company came right out of the blue. I'd like to think about it. They have some wonderful actors and some very good young ones coming up. I could be of great influence there."

"So you're not set on going back to England, Fee?" Brod asked, waiting on her answer.

She looked pensive for a moment. "You know I always said I'd come home when my time in the limelight was over. I still have a name but I think it's time to do something different. If only I could persuade my dearest Fran to join me but she loves her life in England. She loves her father and all their family connections. She gets invited everywhere. She's madly popular."

"I thought she seemed a little disenchanted with her life as it is," Brod mused. "Or maybe that was only the effect Grant was having on her. If you ask me, Fran stole his heart when she was sixteen years old and you brought her on a visit."

"That's right!" Fee said, her face lighting up with a smile. "But Grant's got problems with Fran being who she is, if you know what I mean. Lady Francesca de Lyle."

"Absolutely," Brod agreed. "He knows the sort of life Fran's been used to. She's beautiful, rich, titled, the darling of the society columns. An English rose that could never be transplanted in our wild horizons."

"But, darling," Fee protested, "aren't you forgetting, our own Cecilia was born to a privileged life and she became one of the most admired pioneering women of her time."

"Aw, shucks, Fee," Brod said breezily, "so she did." He walked to the door and sketched a little salute. "I'll be back to collect you around four, Rebecca. You know to wear a good sun-block. There'll be plenty of heat left in the sun."

"Will we be taking the horses?" she asked, lifting her chin a little as she spoke. Since that fateful day and the added shock of hearing the mare, Jeeba, had had to be put down, she found herself oddly reluctant to ride.

In fact she had only ridden out three times since and that was because Ally had especially asked her.

Brod studied her squarely. "We'll be going a good distance so we'll take the Jeep. We might get around to discussing your little problem on the way. I don't want it to turn into a complex."

"Slight exaggeration, Brod," she said sweetly.

"Good." He nodded his approval. "I'd like to go riding with you now and then. You haven't lived until you've had a night out under the desert stars."

"Lordy, no!" Fee put both hands beneath her chin. "Marvellous fun! Of course you're going to need a chaperone."

Brod gave her a wicked grin. "I'll treat that as a joke, Fee."

It was a dream landscape. An endless shimmering ocean of wildflowers rolling over the plains so prolifically the bright red clay was all but hidden. It was a pageantry of flowers the likes of which Rebecca had never thought to see. White, gold, purple, pink, the papery ephemeral flora of this vast mulga region, which bridged the gap between the channel country and the true desert heart, with its glittering mosaic of gibber plains and rising pyramids of sand dunes.

"Enjoy it while you can," Brod said, holding her by the shoulders. "It's only going to last a few weeks then the earth will dry up again."

Rebecca felt her heart expand with delight. "It's a fantastic sight! Magnificent. I feel like I've landed in Paradise."

"All the more breathtaking because it only happens after heavy rains, which could mean once or twice in a year or two. Most of the time it's brilliant blue skies, searing sun and hot drying winds,'' Brod said.

"Wonderland!" Rebecca breathed. "I'd love to pick some to remind me."

"Why not." He smiled indulgently. "Stick to the everlastings—they retain their shape and colour for weeks after. They don't need water, either."

"How extraordinary!" Rebecca swung to face him, transformed from an ice maiden into the vivacious young woman she had once been. "How can anywhere that can produce a glorious show like this be called a desert?"

"You're wonderful," he said, suddenly bending to kiss her mouth. "You're like the seeds of the dormant wildflowers waiting to spring to life."

"That's because you've bedazzled me," she said, unable to hide her feelings.

"I think we've bedazzled each other." He drew her fully into his arms letting his mouth trace all over her face, savouring her scent and her skin, until it came to rest on the soft, silky cushion of her lips. His ardour conveyed powerfully his deep running desire. When he released her neither of them spoke, not wanting to allow a single errant word into their magic circle. It was joy. Incredible joy and a mind-spinning passion.

"Brod," she said, after a moment. "Broderick." She loved the sound of his name on her tongue.

"That's me." His eyes moved over her like blue fire. "What's your second name? You've never told me when I distinctly recall telling you and talking to you just about an entire night."

"It's very prim."

"When you're living such a fast life?" he gently

mocked. "Amy? Emily? I just don't believe you're a Dorothy."

"Actually it's Ellen after an aunt."

"It should have been Eve." His eyes were full of lazy sensuality. He took her hand, leading her down from the vantage point into the shining sea of wildflowers. "We'll avoid that mob of emus to our left," he said. "They're having a great time now with so much herbage around but they can survive in the most arid areas."

Rebecca followed his gaze, feeling her small hand swallowed up in his. Though it was a common sight now to see the great flightless birds, Rebecca found them fascinating especially when running. She knew emus could reach great speeds over rough country. The kangaroos equally fascinating would appear in large mobs about dusk, bounding away on their long hind legs. In the heat of the day they sought the shelter of caves or dense shrub, avoiding unnecessary action and water loss. It was a pattern of behaviour developed over countless thousands of years. But the birds were out as usual in great flocks showing alternate clouds of brilliant colour from backs, wings and undersurfaces. Even as they moved near, vivid mulga parrots landed in a hollow of one of the curious stunted acacias that rose above the vast sea of everlastings showing no alarm at their presence.

Brod went first, gathering a bunch of white everlastings that he fashioned quite skilfully into a garland, placing it on her bare head. "Show me."

Rebecca straightened, eyes luminous, her dark hair escaping in a long, loose outcurving wave to fall across one cheek. She put up a hand to sweep it back but he said rather oddly. "No, leave it." Such an expression was in his eyes Rebecca felt her own vision blur and her limbs turn weak with longing.

"Imagine what you'd look like as a bride."

A bride. She could have cried aloud with the pity of it.

How that marvellous expression would fade if she told him the truth. She'd been a bride. She'd worn the pure shining dress, the long veil that had lent an unearthly radiance to her face. She had looked up at her handsome groom standing before the flower-decked altar with dreams in her eyes. She thought she had seen an answering dream in the intensity of the gaze he had bent on her. The same man who had caused her such misery and pain.

Almost in a twinkling her dazzling pleasure in the day was diminished. How could she ever tell Brod what had happened to her. She couldn't even tell him she had once been married, though he would have known she wasn't a virgin. Surely he might have expected that but she knew in her heart the fact that she had been married without ever revealing it would come as the final blow to his trust.

"No answer?" Now he spoke to her, tracking through the wealth of wildflowers, staring at her stricken face. "I thought every woman wanted to be a bride?" he asked quizzically.

"Well of course!" she realised the error of her reaction. Perhaps he would see what was there in her past.

"Well I'll be damned," he said gently. "Are you frightened of marriage, Rebecca?" He desperately wanted to overcome the huge shift in her mood.

"It's an enormous gamble, Brod. Everyone knows it," she said, tense as a wire.

"But when it works, marriage is so wonderfully rewarding. Most people try it. I thought your parents' marriage was happy despite the fact your mother never recovered from her accident?''

"They were devoted," Rebecca whispered.

"But you agonise about your mother's fate?"

"I'd give anything to have her back." Rebecca looked down at the colourful posy in her hand.

"That's exactly how Ally and I felt about our mother," he said. "I suppose our experiences are proof of our far from happy childhood. Ally apparently couldn't face marriage to Rafe despite the fact she was and I believe still is deeply in love with him."

"And you?" She raised her eyes a long way and stared into his marvellous face.

"I've had casual affairs, Rebecca—" he shrugged "—but I've tried to be scrupulously honest with the women in my life. Marriage is a very different thing from a romance. When I choose a wife I'm going to take darn good care I find the right woman. I've had my life torn apart once. It's not going to happen again."

She felt exactly the same way.

They were quiet on the return trip; Brod stunned to discover the passionate young woman he now knew Rebecca to be could genuinely be disturbed by the thought of marriage. Hadn't he seen something like horror expressed in her face back there? Perhaps someone had hurt her badly? Someone about whom she refused to speak. Feeling as he did, he would have to give her time. He understood now the "coolness" of the facade she had cultivated. It was all about throwing up defences. Defences he now realised he badly wanted to break down.

"Where are we going?" Rebecca asked some time later into the quietness. They had been driving for miles yet the flowers went on, the everlastings turning to carpets of snow, native poppies and hibiscus, undulating seas of green pussy tails, lilac fan flowers, the flaming fire bush, the salt bush and the cotton bush and the spreading Opomoea. This wasn't the legendary Dead Heart that had claimed so many victims, it was the biggest garden on earth. The Jeep left the flower smothered plains heading towards a dense line of green, which could only mean a lagoon or rock pool was feeding it.

"I want you to see my favourite swimming pool," Brod said. "That's when the time is right. We'll have to stop soon and walk the rest of the way. It's a glorious place. It even has a little waterfall."

"I think I can hear it," Rebecca said, aware of rushing sounds. As they drove closer she was certain. Tumbling water. It sounded marvellous in the glittering heat. Brod stopped the Jeep in the shade of the trees and switched off the engine.

"It's a bit of a way down. Are you up to it?" His eyes gleamed.

"Of course I am!" A growing excitement was reigniting her spirits.

"You won't be sorry...I promise you."

He held her hand all the way, holding back branches in case they whipped at her face or body; stopping when she became a little puffed. Finally, when they had almost reached the bottom of the slope crowded with white spider lilies in their thousands, he picked her up and carried her the rest of the way. When she exclaimed at the beauty of this secret spot he lowered her gently to her feet.

"But this is...ravishing." Rebecca was thrilled by the tranquil beauty of the pool and the much cooler atmosphere. From high up among the trees a small silvery waterfall tumbled over rocks and into the pool, which was shaded at the edges a pale jade, emerald in the depths. A place for lovers, she thought. Paradise before the Fall. A beautiful quiet secret place with the scent of a million wildflowers held in suspension in the golden green air.

"I knew you'd like it," Brod said, delighted by her expression.

"I love it. Does anyone come here?"

"Only me. Ally, too, when we were kids. There are dozens of lagoons to swim in on Kimbara. This is my private place. No one comes here. Not even the cattle. Probably no one even knows about it and I'm not about to tell them."

"*I* know," she boasted.

"So you can see, you're honoured."

Rebecca turned away, overcome by her feelings. As a kind of respite she bent to an exquisite little flower that grew in an isolated clump beside a rock.

"What's this?" She fingered a delicate mauve petal.

He glanced down. "I've no idea. There are so many beautiful nameless flowers tucked away."

"Name it after me." She looked up and let her eyes linger.

"I know what." His voice was deep and indulgent. "Rebecca Lily. You have the same delicate air."

"Okay. You stick to that. Rebecca Lily. Is that a promise?"

"It's Rebecca Lily forever as far as I'm concerned."

She stayed where she was and undid the laces of her shoes. "I'm going to paddle."

He let her go, watching her slender figure clad in pink cotton jeans and a matching shirt move across the sandy bank to the crystal clear water. Now she was standing in ankle deep, tugging at the hem of her jeans. "Crazy!" she called. "We should have brought our swimsuits."

Desire swept through him like a fire through dry grass. He had wanted her long before he had actually known her beautiful body. Now that he had it was an everyday battle just to keep his hands off her. His need for her was immense, the strength of it gaining with every passing day.

"Brod?" she ran back to him laughing, the water she had splashed so lavishly all over her face glistening on her magnolia skin, running down her neck into her pink shirt, wetting it so it clung to her breasts. His eyes tracked the water's progress. She wasn't wearing a bra. He could see the naked sensitised nipples peaking against the sodden material. It was too much. Too much. He was a desiring man and he couldn't stand it.

"We could always take off our clothes," he suggested very softly, drawing her to him by the collar of her shirt, letting his hands move to the top button.

"I'm too modest." Yet she leaned into him, tingling cascades of sensation running down her spine.

"When I've kissed every inch of your beautiful body?" That memory would stay with him forever.

"At least I had the cover of moonlight," she whispered, beginning to tremble.

"You didn't in the dawn." When he had taken her without speaking.

"When I had to leave you."

"I've never let a beautiful woman visit me in my bedroom before," he told her, looking deeply into her eyes.

"I'm the only one?"

"I mean what I tell you." His vibrant voice was

deep. He began to undo the little pearly pink buttons one by one giving her all the time in the world to draw back, watching her intoxicated, the stars in her eyes. Finally he peeled it off her like the petals of a flower. At her little affirming cry he swooped like a falcon out of a clear cobalt sky pulling her unstoppably into his arms and planting his deeply desiring kiss on her mouth.

She might have been a violin in the hands of a master, her whole body one sweet seamless vibrato. She craved his embrace, revelled in it. It was almost as if this place was watching over them. The encircling trees, the broad sweep of spider lilies, the ancient rocks, the emerald pool, sparkling waterfall, the swarm of iridescent insects that hovered over a blossoming shrub with a waxy flower that resembled a native frangipani.

The spirit of the bush. She had to glory in every moment.

On a rippling tide of emotion, Rebecca broke away from him, her eyes like liquid diamonds. She tilted her head back, laughing aloud with pure joy, the action lifting her small breasts and tautening her creamy torso so her ribs showed. "I want to swim in the pool," she announced blissfully.

"I want to dive off the ledge and touch the sand at the bottom. I want to swim several lengths then for a finale I'm going to jump up on that flat rock out there and sun-bake until I'm dry." Without hesitation or the slightest show of self-consciousness she slid off the rest of her clothes, jeans and briefs then took long springing steps, gazellelike, into the clear sheet of water.

"Listen I'm ready to join you," Brod called, the lightness of his tone belying the mounting intensity that was in him. His hands swiftly stripped off his denim shirt and moved to the silver buckle of his leather belt.

This woman, this incredibly beautiful naked nymph kept transforming herself. One moment one thing, something different the next. Every image fresh and new. She was creating something approaching a delicious frenzy in his blood.

Soon he was stripped of his clothes, his lean powerful body deeply tanned all over, the dappled sunlight playing over gleaming skin and long, taut muscles. He could hear her calling to him, as alluring as a siren who lived in the emerald depths, lifting her arm to beckon.

"It's wonderful, wonderful," she cried. "So cold I can't stand it."

She'd warm up, he vowed, moving into a smooth, powerful dive. My God she would! He'd make love to her until she was on fire. Utterly his.

Stock mustering and drafting went on at a back-breaking pace. One of Kimbara's top stockmen, Curly Jenkins, miraculously escaped serious injury when during the course of the drafting at Leura Creek a mob of bullocks broke free and crashed through an iron gate leaving the unfortunate Curly crushed behind it. Brod, who was at the homestead when the accident occurred, had the news from Curly's offsider who rode at breakneck speed to the homestead to give the alarm. Brod immediately contacted the Flying Doctor who flew Curly out to hospital suffering, as was confirmed, from badly bruised ribs, and severe bruising to the trunk. Less than a week later Grant Cameron called on Brod to join in a ground search for one of his helicopter pilots who had begun mustering cattle on one of the Cameron outstations but had not called in at the end of the day. Grant had been unable to reach him by the company radio and

the pilot had not cancelled his SAR, his search and rescue time.

At first no one was all that worried; Grant himself
said radio problems weren't that unusual. The pilot, an
experienced man, could simply have landed somewhere
and set up camp for the night. He had his swag aboard.

The men searched all day with no luck. First light the
following morning the search was stepped up to full
scale with planes and helicopters retracing the pilot's
course. Brod flew the Beech Baron and Rebecca, caught
up in the now general anxiety, begged to go along as a
spotter. It was her first time flying with Brod but this
wasn't the exciting joy trip it might have been. It was
she who first saw the wreckage, distressing her terribly,
scant moments before Brod who began circling the area
pinpointed the fatal spot. A short time later the rescue
helicopter arrived to land on the difficult terrain.

The fatality affected everyone. The pilot was well-
known and liked reminding them of the dangers that
were a normal part of station life. Rebecca began to
find it very difficult not to dwell on Brod's safety. There
was hardly a day he and his staff weren't challenged.
Rebecca had watched him on a motorbike mustering a
herd of bullocks with her heart in her mouth. Then there
was all the flying he began to do to the outstations and
other Kinross stations in the chain. Over vast distances
the only way to go was by air. Rebecca found herself
fighting anxiety until he was safely back.

"Darling, Brod is a wonderful pilot," Fee reassured
her. "A natural. He's had his licence for years. It's es-
sential in his job.

Still Rebecca prayed.

CHAPTER EIGHT

IT WAS an idyll that had to end. Rebecca was to learn the past is never past. It keeps coming back at you.

Up in the pre-dawn Brod left Fee a reminder their financial people, accountants and tax solicitors would be flying in for a meeting that afternoon. In all likelihood it could spin out to the next day. Four in all. Barry Mattheson and his associate and Dermot Shields was bringing someone, too. He had given instructions to Jean to make up the guest rooms just in case.

"I can't bear talking money," Fee moaned, "but I'm involved in it all. Sir Andy left me with a lot of clout. He wasn't going to give it all to Stewart. His affairs will take *ages* to finalise."

"Well I've got plenty to keep me busy," Rebecca said, folding her napkin and rising from the breakfast table. "In fact, we're moving along very nicely, Fee. This is going to be a winner. A marvellous read."

"I won't be glad when it's over." Fee, who was still seated finishing off a cup of tea, caught Rebecca's hand. "I've loved having you here, darling, and Brod is happier than I've ever seen him in his life. Close as we are I'm giving you *all* the credit for that. Would you come around here, girl, so I can see you?" Fee teased.

Colouring Rebecca moved back giving Fee a little bob. "Yes m'lady." She tried to speak gaily, but emotion throbbed in her voice.

"You're in love with him aren't you?" Fee asked

151

very gently, retaining Rebecca's hand and staring up into her transparent face.

"I thought I knew what love was," Rebecca said dreamily. "I didn't. This time I do. Every time I see him my heart sings, Beloved! I can't describe what I feel for him as anything other than sublime." Her beautiful eyes suddenly glittered with unshed tears.

"Have you told him any of this?" Fee was enthralled.

"Not in so many words," Rebecca confessed. "I couldn't bear to tell him about my life."

Fee looked alarmed. "Darling girl, you're making it sound horrifying."

Rebecca's luminous grey eyes darkened to pewter. "I'd give anything for a lot of it not to have happened, Fee," she said, gravely.

"Do you want to tell me?" the older woman urged, quite concerned. "Goodness I really do feel like your aunt."

"I mean to tell you, Fee," Rebecca decided. "But I must tell Brod first."

"Of course," Fee murmured. "My every instinct was you've had a bad experience in life even if you do look exquisite."

"I've been hiding myself away," Rebecca said. "I don't mean literally. I've seen a lot, done a lot. Had my success. It hasn't been easy but I thought that was what I had to do."

"But you've talked about your family. Of your love for your mother and father and your family in Hong Kong." Fee continued to look up at her with concern.

"It's something else, Fee. Someone I met when I was very young. And on my own."

"Well I know all about that," Fee confided in her

wonderfully expressive voice. Forty years later still with faint bitterness. "All I can tell you, dear, is it will be much better to get whatever it is out in the open. Tell Brod. It will only get harder as more time passes."

"I know." Rebecca gave a little shudder.

Fee shook her head. "Don't be too nervous, Rebecca," she warned. "Maybe I should tell you Ally said Brod was madly in love with you before she left. Take into account that upsetting little experience with my poor brother. Brod felt it badly. My advice is, darling, and I've got a lot of insider knowledge, don't keep any secrets from Brod."

"I won't!"

If it kills me, Rebecca thought.

Brod dashed in for a quick shower and a change of clothes before Barry Mattheson and party were due in at Kimbara's airstrip.

"I'll make myself scarce," Rebecca said, standing on the staircase, looking over her shoulder to speak to him as he was making for the door.

"Stay and meet them," he invited with a smile.

"No, I'll let you all get on with it. I have plenty to do."

"Well you'll meet them all at dinner." Brod shrugged. "We've got one hell of a lot to sort out. I doubt we can get through it all this afternoon."

"Take care." She blew him a kiss.

"I mean to," he said.

For you. He wasn't pushing Rebecca even when he was crazy about her but he intended to take their relationship a whole lot further. Like an engagement. Pretty soon after that she was going to become his beautiful bride. Despite herself. He was going to do everything in his power to make his wife happy.

Rebecca!

He started down the steps filled with incredible life and vigour.

Rebecca heard the visitors arrive but she made no effort to go to the window and look out. She kept working, realising she was almost at the point of making a first draft of Fee's biography. Fee, in her private conversations, was always very honest; now that same honesty had been extended to the book. In Rebecca's opinion, it was turning into a rather extraordinary chronicle, not only Fee's life but the Kinross family life down through the generations. She knew it would be every bit as good as Dame Judith's memoirs, which had received excellent reviews. It was nice to get praise. One reviewer had referred to her "elegant, even lyrical prose." She hoped it was matched by realism. Fee had entrusted her with quite a commission. This would be a bigger and better book than Dame Judith's because there was so much more to say about a long line of extraordinary characters.

Fee tapped on her door around six, her beautiful face touched with exhaustion.

"How's it going?" Rebecca asked, sounding concerned. "It's been a long session."

"That it has!" Fee put a hand to her temple. "Sir Andy used to have a small army of lawyers. At least we've cut it down a bit. All I can say is it's damned fortunate Brod is so clever. He's right up with them. Doesn't miss a single solitary thing. I get bogged down a bit. We used to have an enormous fortune you know.

It's mind-boggling how much Stewart got through. Lived like a prince while Brod handled everything from the minute he was able to.''

"Are you going to come in and sit down?" Rebecca asked. "You look a little tired."

"I am, darling," Fee confessed, "but I'll keep you company at dinner."

"Good. I didn't want to be the only woman there. What are they like?"

Fee glanced at her watch. "Well I've known dear old Barry since forever. I knew his father before him. Dermot is a new one on me but sounds like a good man. The other two are much younger but very bright. Early thirties. I'll go off now and soak in a long, luxurious bath.

"Do you good." Rebecca gave her an affectionate smile and turned back to the word processor. She'd work for another half hour or so then draw her own bath.

She took her time when she was usually eager to go downstairs, selecting a two-piece jersey outfit in her favourite colour, violet, probably because it looked good on her. It had a simple high-necked sleeveless top and a long fluid skirt, which she wore well. Some of her girl-friends thought you had to be tall to wear long skirts. She found just the opposite. They actually made her look taller and she liked the sensual feel of soft fabrics against her legs.

Her hair was getting very long. She hadn't had it cut for months. She parted it in the centre and brushed it to a high glow, pushing it behind her ears and letting it flow down her back. Next diamond stud earrings she had bought herself to mark her New Journalist of the

Year award. A few swishes of O de Lancôme—she was never without it—and she was ready.

All through the afternoon, even when she was working on the book, her conversation with Fee stayed at the back of her mind. No doubt getting it all out into the open was good advice but her extreme reluctance was proof how badly she had been traumatised.

Rebecca sank into a gold brocade armchair burying her head in her hands for a moment.

"Brod," she rehearsed in her mind, "there's something about me I haven't told you...."

"Brod, I've wanted to tell you this for so long but..."

"Brod, I've been married. Years ago. To a violent man. Well he wasn't violent at the beginning. He used to be so nice... Nice, God!"

"Brod, I married a charming, unpredictable man."

It was going to be a terrible shock his finding out. Their relationship, never casual, had escalated so rapidly into a grand love affair all the more extraordinary because neither of them had put their deepest feelings into words. In a way both of them had a problem saying, "I love you," though Brod told her the most beautiful things about herself unable to hide his desire and need.

What a ghastly mess she'd made of it all. It was now imperative she speak out. If she left it any longer she would lose him. This man who had given her back her dreams. This man who put so much store in trusting. In a way she had been leading a double life. Now she would have to face reality.

Rebecca stood up and went to the mirror, looking deeply into her reflected eyes. "Go on, do it. I dare you. Tell Brod about this man he has never heard of. Your husband. Your ex-husband who liked to hurt you. Tell him about your husband's mother, the real head of the family, who would never hear a word against her perfect son. Go on. Tell him. And tell him very soon.''

Rebecca smiled ruefully at herself, feeling better. There was no crime in having been married. Her only sin was not telling the man she loved.

Moments later while she was waiting for half past seven when she would go downstairs, Brod came to collect her wearing a soft open-necked blue shirt with grey trousers and a summer weight navy blazer trimmed with gold buttons. She had always thought him as stunning, burning with life, but with whatever had happened between them his looks were positively hypnotic, this man with the wonderful blue eyes.

''Hi!'' she said, her heart thudding beneath the thin violet jersey.

''That's nice,'' he said in a low voice his gaze moving very slowly over her. ''Purple is definitely your colour.''

''How was your day?'' she asked.

''Not completely satisfactory.'' He rubbed the back of his neck as if to ease it. ''But we're working on it.'' He took another glance at her mouth. ''I'd love to kiss you. I mean I want to kiss you all the time really, but we'd better go downstairs.'' He put out a hand, unable to resist sliding it down her satiny waterfall of hair. ''I like your hair longer. It's perfect parted in the centre.''

''I aim to please you,'' she said, feeling a bit intoxicated.

''You *do?*''

''What do you think, Brod?'' She lifted her dark head to him. ''I've gone to pieces over you.''

He laughed; a flash of beautiful white teeth. ''Gone to pieces of course. But are you in love with me?''

''You don't believe me?''

"Yes, but I'm not exactly sure what yes means. I'd really like to know what you want of me, Rebecca?"

"Nothing. Everything," she said.

He moved her back against the wall, bent his head, just barely grazing her mouth, but the effect was sizzling, robbing her of breath. "You're a magnet for me."

She stared into his eyes. "I know so much about you. So much about your family. You know so little about me."

"I thought you were going to tell me everything one day," he challenged.

She frowned, very serious. "I want to tell you *tonight*."

If it were possible the colour in his sapphire eyes deepened. "Rebecca, you little Sphinx, I'll be waiting for you."

As they walked to the head of the staircase, Fee, who had been playing hostess, came out into the Front Hall, looking amazingly rich and famous. "Ah, there you are, my darlings. Jean has dinner ready for eight. "You'll want a pre-dinner drink."

The four men who had been seated in the drawing room, a pleasant relaxed group, now came to their feet, wondering who the beautiful young woman was on Brod's arm.

Three were wondering.

One had no reason to. He already knew Rebecca Hunt. He knew she had been commissioned to write Fiona Kinross's biography. He'd seen it in the papers. Rebecca had become more successful than he ever would have given her credit for. Now she was happily at home with these megarich people. These top people. This great landed family. Who could beat that?

Rebecca totally unprepared thought she might faint

from the shock. It was amazing she *didn't* faint, her vision had become so blurred. But she would have known him anywhere. Martyn Osborne. Her ex-husband.

Dear God she pleaded inwardly. Don't punish me any more.

Brod, about to make the introductions, became aware of the tiniest little flutters in Rebecca's body, the quickening of her breath. Something was perturbing her. He looked down at her face swiftly and saw it confident, exquisitely poised. She wore the smooth mask he had almost forgotten. The shields were down. But he knew something was very wrong.

Speak to him as though you've never seen him before in your life, was Rebecca's first frantic thought. Play a role. Be as brilliant as Fee. She had nothing to be ashamed of. It was Martyn who ought to be deeply ashamed. There was no way she was going to fear him any more.

She got a vague impression of the older men. One silver haired, distinguished, the other portly, the younger man almost a matched pair with Martyn. Fair, well-bred, good looks and near identical smart casual clothing. Martyn had obviously left his old legal firm to join Mattheson & Mattheson. Another good career move. It was an incredibly bizarre situation but one she had to get through. The decision taken, she moved smoothly into speech, countering her turmoil with courage. Just too ridiculous to pretend she didn't know him at all.

"But, Martyn, what a surprise!" she exclaimed, with mild pleasure. "Martyn and I were at university together." She looked to Brod and Fee in explanation. "I swear it's a small world." At least *that* was true.

"How nice!" Fee stared at her, not in the least fooled, even if she applauded the acting.

He'd thought she'd be struck dumb with shock, possibly make an utter fool of herself, yet here she was extending her hand, withdrawing it very promptly before he had a chance to tighten his grasp. "How are you, Martyn?" she asked, feeling his eyes eating into her.

"Fine, Becky. Never better. Someone was only talking about you the other day. It was my mother actually. Why don't you call her?"

Because she disgusts me. Like you. "Lord, I'm terrible keeping up with all my phone calls," she answered lightly, allowing Brod to move her on to the leader of the group. Barry Mattheson responded with genuine pleasure, remarking on Rebecca's professional success. "I've had the pleasure of reading your biography of Dame Judith Thomas," he said. "My wife read it first and gave it to me. Both of us thoroughly enjoyed it."

"You won't have to buy a copy of mine, Barry," Fee told him, patting his arm. "I'll be sending you and Dolly an autographed copy."

"I'll hold you to that, Fee."

The portly Dermot Shields came next, his good-natured face intelligent and alert. Jonathan Reynolds, Dermot Shields' aide stood to attention, impeccably groomed and a little overawed by the grandeur of his surroundings. This was the first time Jonathan had ever visited one of the country's great historic homesteads and he was mightily impressed.

By the time they went into dinner it was apparent to Rebecca Martyn was going to play along with her. At least for the time being. She knew he was quite capable of denouncing her the moment he saw fit. Perhaps he was hording the pleasure. Or quick-witted at all times he had divined Brod's interest in her and as a consequence was trying to work out how best to proceed.

Destroy her or maybe make a big career error, Martyn Osborne thought, taking his place at the big gleaming dinner table with its swanky appointments. The Kinross family were at the top of his firm's long list of wealthy clients. He had even thought with secret contempt old Mattheson positively worshipped them. It would be incredibly stupid to upset this lot. Or be seen to be upsetting them deliberately.

He had noticed Kinross's swift reactions on his oh so superior face. Handsome as the devil with that shock of blue-black hair, too damned long—who did he think he was…Mel Gibson?—and those startling blue eyes. What an arrogant bastard he was. Of course he was in love with Becky. Imagine she was more beautiful than ever with a cool poise that was entirely new to him. He'd given her so much and it meant nothing to her. He'd loved her too much and she had twisted that love. Turned him into someone else. It was all her fault. Everything. He had never forgiven her. He had never got over it.

Carrying a deep grudge all these years. He'd worked hard to manoeuvre himself into the position to accompany old Mattheson on this trip, never for a moment volunteering the knowledge he knew his ex-wife was on Kimbara helping that over-the-hill actress, Fiona Kinross, to write her silly memoirs.

Mattheson knew he had been married of course. Knew the marriage had ended in divorce but he had no idea his ex-wife was Rebecca Hunt. Needless to say Beck would revert to her maiden name just to spite him. He wanted to give her a bad time, but wanted to be able

to think of the best way to go about it. He'd like to
shake that acting cool and banish the gleam in Kinross's
blue eyes every time he looked at her. The worst bitterness was he still wanted his ex-wife. Wasn't that the
reason for pursuing her out to this godforsaken wilderness?

Rebecca went through dinner in a trance of some sort,
somehow holding to her end of the conversation, a little
slow to answer Martyn's trick questions. He's crazy, she
thought. Nothing to indicate it. He's handsome; very
correct in his behaviour. Charming to Fee. Just the right
amount of deference when speaking to Brod and his
senior colleagues, a touch patronising with Jonathan
Reynolds who was totally lacking in Martyn's over-
weening self-confidence. Nicely friendly with her. Old
chums from way back exchanging light conversation.

Except for his eyes. She could see the malice in them.
The venom. She tried to understand how she had ever
come to marry him. But then she had known nothing
about the dark side of men.

Brod for his part, decided to say nothing. He allowed
Rebecca to carry on with this charade. He was so close
to her now, so at *one* with her he knew under the polished facade disturbance ran deep. Without appearing
to in the least he kept Osborne under close scrutiny.
Osborne, too, was doing his best to cover the feelings
that were rife in him but Brod knew his instincts were
right. Even during the flow of conversation he kept turning things over in his mind. He was beginning to believe
this smooth-faced lawyer with his faintly pompous demeanour and his small mannerisms, the little twitch of
the eyebrows, the restless hands, the fake laugh, was
the man who had brought much unhappiness into
Rebecca's life.

Becky, he called her. Not surrounding the sharpness

of the word with cushioning grace. It sat oddly with Rebecca's delicate appearance. Brod understood there was a story there. He intended to find out about it. He hadn't liked Osborne from the moment he had met him. Somehow Osborne had struck him as a malicious schoolboy. Just a fancy but long experience had taught him he had little need to question his judgement.

A malicious schoolboy. One who liked to pick the wings off butterflies.

They lingered over coffee, taking it out onto the verandah at Fee's suggestion so they could enjoy the welcome coolness of the night and the glorious vault of the heavens filled with a billion glittering stars. Nowhere did they sparkle so brilliantly or in such infinite numbers as over the rarefied air of the desert.

It was Barry Mattheson who suggested to his colleagues they should turn in. Martyn turned to Rebecca. "Once around the garden, Becky, for old times' sake. I haven't gotten around to telling you about some of our old friends. Remember Sally Griffiths and her sister? Dinah Marshall? They've set up their own school for gifted kids. Doing well to. Gordon Clark? He was mad about you. Weren't they all!"

You included, Brod thought, wanting to pull Rebecca into his protective arms,

But she wanted to go with Osborne. "I've got a little time to catch up." She stood to join Martyn, knowing she had little alternative. Because of the conversation at the dinner table, Martyn knew for certain now both Brod and Fee believed her to be a single woman. Fee had even commented Rebecca would make some man the perfect wife one day. "We'll be ten minutes no more," she told Brod. "I know you like to lock up."

In fact Brod never locked up. Who was there to raid him? This was his own kingdom.

Fee, her antennae working overtime, felt driven to whisper to Brod, "Keep an eye on her, darling. There's something about that young man I don't like."

"I'm going to," Brod confirmed grimly. "I can recognise menace when I see it."

"Poor little Rebecca!" Fee said, her heart sinking. "She's hiding something, Brod."

"Don't I know!" Brod's expression was taut. "I can't tell you *what* exactly but she's very disturbed."

When their guests retired, Brod kept Rebecca and Martyn under silent surveillance, moving soundlessly along the length of the side verandah, then moving out into the darkened garden all the while listening to the murmur of their voices. This was something he had never done in his life—eavesdrop—but he had no compunction about doing it now. He knew something was badly wrong. He knew the two of them had been playing along.

Until *now* when they thought themselves alone.

As they moved further away from the house, Martyn clamped his hand around Rebecca's arm but she freed herself by jerking away forcefully. "It wouldn't be good for you if I started to scream," she warned in a soft, furious voice. "Brod would pound the life out of you."

"He'd have a go," he scoffed, secretly hating to have to put it to the test.

"The hell he would!" Rebecca said with disgust. "He's head and shoulders over you. And I mean in every way."

"In love with him, are you?" he sneered, all the old memories flooding back. His jealous rages.

"You don't need to know," Rebecca replied quietly.

"Oh, yes, I *do!*"

"You need help, Martyn. You always did."

He wasn't about to listen to that. Women with the way they twisted things. "Nothing would ever have gone wrong between us except for you," he hissed.

Their voices were pitched deliberately low but Brod caught it. His suspicions confirmed. No surprise. This was the man in Rebecca's life.

"What is it exactly you *want*, Martyn?" Rebecca asked.

"Can't you see. I want you back. Everything that happened was your fault."

"You need to believe that," Rebecca observed wearily. "Like I said you need help."

"I engineered this trip out here," he told her, a kind of triumph in his voice. "Saw in the paper some time ago you were working on a new biography. Fiona Kinross. Fate with just a little jump start from me let you fall into my hands. I knew all about our Kinross clients. Big. *Very big.* Next thing there's a trip scheduled for Kimbara. Another associate was lined up to go but I'm good at manoeuvring."

Are you indeed, Brod thought, moving ever closer.

Again Rebecca's voice sounded inexpressibly tired of it all. "What could you hope to possibly gain? If you were the last man on earth I'd never come back to you."

I'd never let you.

"That's put another knife through my heart," Osborne burst out.

"You haven't got a heart, Martyn. You've just got a big inflated ego."

"So what's the plan?" Osborne demanded. "Kinross? Are you after him? You always were a high flier."

Listening Brod clenched his fist.

"You mean when I settled for you." Rebecca's voice was icy with contempt.

"My family aren't any ordinary family," Osborne bragged. "We're very well connected. That was a big inducement for you. Do you think I don't know that?"

She tried to swallow. "Martyn, I'm going back. You still talk more rubbish than I've ever heard in my life."

He caught her shoulder. "I'll make you pay. I swear it."

"Do your worst." This from Rebecca, as she flung away.

"Whatever *that* could possibly be," Brod suddenly appeared on the path before them. In the faint light from the verandah he looked very tall, powerfully built, very angry. "You're a visitor here in my house, Osborne," he grated. "It appears to me you're harassing Rebecca. I'm here to help her."

Osborne seemed to gasp for breath. "Harassing?" He sounded shocked, wounded. "Believe me, Mr. Kinross, that's the last thing I would do. You've got it all wrong."

"Have I? Rebecca, come over here." Brod indicated with his arm where Rebecca should stand. Beside him. "Then I think you ought to explain. You've been goading Rebecca all night. I'm not a fool."

"A fool. That's the last thing I'd say you were." Osborne's confident voice wobbled. "I was shocked out of my mind when I saw Becky here. How would I ever know?"

"You'd better tell me," Brod invited pretending he didn't already know.

"He read I was here in the newspaper," Rebecca supplied, not daring to look up at Brod's steely profile. "He managed to convince Mr. Mattheson he was the best person to bring."

"Why exactly," Brod asked.

"If you only knew." Osborne suddenly clutched his head with his hands giving every impression of a man driven by grief to speak out. "Is it a crime to try to get your wife back?"

"Dear God!" Rebecca burst out imploringly to an indifferent heavens. Brod, totally off guard, reeled back as if taking a king hit. The bliss of these past weeks was smashed into the ground. Trust destroyed. The madness was she had brought it all on her own head. She understood it all. One terrible mistake could change a life forever.

"I only want her back." Osborne's low, impassioned voice came again, an assault to Brod's ringing ears. "I love her. I never ceased loving her."

It rang true. Nevertheless, or perhaps because of it, Brod moved suddenly, jerking Osborne forward by the lapels of his jacket. "Wait a minute. You're trying to tell me Rebecca is your wife? You came here to my home to this station to try to effect a reconciliation?"

"I swear I didn't know what else to do." Osborne's voice broke almost in despair. "She refused to see me, answer my letters, my mother's pleas all these years."

"Years? What are we talking about here? She hasn't been with you for years?" Brod sounded very, very, angry.

Rebecca knew Brod probably wouldn't want to hear from her again still she spoke. "Martyn and I were divorced years ago. It was a very unhappy marriage. I never wanted to lay eyes on him again."

Even with the roaring in his ears Brod heard the word divorced, the only word that pulled him back. "I can understand that," he rasped.

"What is a man supposed to do if his wife won't honour her sacred vows?" Osborne's voice throbbed with raw emotion as he held up a hand as if to shield his face.

Yes, I'd like to punch you, Brod thought. I'd like to lay you out cold but I shouldn't because I'm supposed to be a civilised man.

"Damn you for thinking you could start here." Disgustedly Brod let his hands fall. "Let me understand something—" finally, his face grave, he turned on Rebecca "—is there some remote possibility you could go back to this guy?"

She shook her head, wrapping her arms around her. "No." It would be like being driven back into hell.

"Did you hear that?" Brod swung back to Osborne, terse and powerful.

"I just wanted to hear it from her own lips." In the midst of his humiliation Martyn knew a moment of pure triumph. Vengeance was sweet. If there was anything going on between Kinross and Becky—and he was sure that there was—dear little Becky had well and truly blotted her copy book. What was the old saying? Second hand goods. A man like Kinross wouldn't want a woman with the merest hint of scandal in her background. He could beat this up for all it was worth, only chances were it could all rebound on him. Better to play the poor fool. "Can you blame me for loving her?" he asked in a quiet, defeated voice. "I'd apologise to you abjectly if it would do me any good."

"It won't," Brod returned, very bluntly. "If I were you I'd go inside and reconsider your position. You came here under false pretences. Do you think I couldn't get you sacked?''

"I'm sure you could." Martyn hung his head. Remorse was the way to go.

"I'm half-way sure I *should*." Brod cut him off, looking at him with cold suspicion. "I may even get around to it if you feel you should spread your story. It wouldn't do anyone any good now. Rebecca has told you there's no chance of any reconciliation. None whatsoever. You'd better accept that. For all time.''

"I know when I'm beaten," Martyn answered. Glad, yes glad to see Becky so stricken. He wanted her to understand he could still reach out and hurt her. "But surely you can find it in your heart to forgive my coming here? For acting the way I have? Rebecca promised to marry me till death do us part. That meant everything to me. In the end it meant nothing to her.''

They stood seemingly like statues listening to Martyn's footsteps trudge back to the house.

Brod was the first to break the highly charged silence.

"He can stick to his room tomorrow," he said, his voice still deeply angry. "Tell Barry he's ill. I don't want him privy to any more of my family's affairs. God I can't take it all in even now. I'll tell Barry I want someone else on the job. Someone with more seniority. Barry can think what he likes.''

"I'm sorry, Brod. So sorry.''

He caught her chin, looking down into her shocked face. "Are you? You had no intention of telling me, did you?''

There was a little shift in her shoulders. "You don't really understand. My marriage was a time of great unhappiness. I have great difficulty thinking about it let alone talking about it.''

"To *me?*" He felt cut to the heart. "To the man you've lain with in such intimacy for all these weeks. The man you claimed made you so happy?"

She turned her tear-blinded, shamed face away. "I was afraid to tell you."

"*Why* exactly?" he demanded, filled with disbelief. "Am I some kind of an ogre?"

"You don't trust me, Brod," she said simply. "Underneath it all you've *never* trusted me. You're not completely in love with me as I am with you."

He could scarcely hear her over the thud of his heart. "Ah, don't give me that!" he said in a contemptuous rush. "I've been waiting for you to speak to me. I've been so patient. I've given you plenty of time. I'm not a patient man."

"I love you." She stared up at him as if committing his face to memory.

He laughed, even now feeling a deep well of desire. "You're saying this *now*. How long was it going to take you? Or were you waiting for me to ask you to marry me?"

"I never believed you would," she said, profoundly fatalistic.

He grasped her by the shoulders as if to shake the life out of her, the brief surge of violence conquered by his natural gallantry towards women.

"You thought you were destined to be my mistress?" He let his hands shape her delicate bones, their strength quietened.

"I've come to believe bad karma might be the pattern of my life. All the agony with my mother, growing up. Praying for her to get better and she never did. My marriage to Martyn. When I look back on it I was just a kid looking for a safe home. I had no one. I visited my father maybe a couple of times a year.''

His eyes showed their bewilderment. ''Is all of this so terrible you couldn't tell me?''

She knew his effort to control his anger with her wouldn't extend to Martyn. And Martyn was still in the house. Brod wouldn't take her story of physical and mental abuse without confronting Martyn with it. A terrible argument would take place. Perhaps Martyn would get what he thoroughly deserved. But at what price? Fee would be terribly upset at such ugliness. Barry Mattheson and his colleagues would be made aware of it, without question.

She didn't know how long she stood there without answering. ''I can only say I'm sorry, Brod.'' Maybe she could redeem herself. But it would have to be another time.

His hands finally came down in rejection. ''Well, sorry, Rebecca, it's not good enough. All this time in your own way you've been lying to me. To Fee. Have you really grown so close to her or is it all an act? I don't understand you at all.''

''I don't understand myself,'' she admitted openly. ''Perhaps I should have counselling.''

''Have you always concealed things, Rebecca?'' He searched her face, pale as a pearl in the brilliant starlight.

''You have to believe I was going to tell you everything tonight.''

He gave a brief torn laugh. ''The truth at last, only your ex-husband, Martyn, beat you to it. I can't say I took to the pompous son of a bitch but I'm damned if I can condemn him. He said he still loves you, Rebecca, I believe him.''

"That's because you don't know the kind of man Martyn really is. He doesn't know what true love means. All he knows is right of possession. As if you can ever own a human being.''

"You don't want to be owned?" he asked quietly.

Now *she* was angry. "I *won't* be owned.''

"You fear entering into another marriage? You think all men are mean and possessive?''

"No, not you." Never you. There was nothing in her beautiful Brod to dread.

"Yet you thought I was totally devoid of human sympathy,'' he said, in a deep, wondering voice. "Loving you and God help me, Rebecca, I do. You thought I couldn't listen to your story. Help you fight all your perceived dark places. You talk about this Martyn, your ex-husband. Well I've got news for you, Rebecca, you don't know what love means, either.''

CHAPTER NINE

BACK in Sydney, Rebecca wrote with obsessive nervous energy, virtually unreachable to her friends. She was on her third draft of Fee's biography. The final copy. The phone rang many times. She never answered it. Who did she have anyway? She kept in touch with her father, Vivienne and the children. Vivienne had been going on about a visit. They hadn't seen her for such a while and they longed to. What about Christmas in Hong Kong?

"I won't give up until I've persuaded you," Vivienne said.

It seemed to Rebecca an ocean separated her from the ones she loved. An ocean of sea. An ocean of desert sand. In the month since she had left Kimbara she and Fee kept in touch but her sense of isolation had deepened terribly. Even Fee hadn't been able to persuade her not to leave. Rebecca frowned to herself, remembering...

"I despise that young man coming out here trying to make trouble." Fee's voice was sharp with denunciation. "Let the dust settle, Rebecca, Brod will come around. Though there's no denying you made a big mistake not telling us, darling. It didn't do anyone any good. You do see that?"

"Of course I do, Fee," Rebecca answered her. "I promised you I'd tell Brod that awful night and I meant to but it was doomed never to work out."

Fee had gazed at her for a long while. "You poor girl! If only you'd come to me for help. Heavens, darling, it's not as though you did something dreadfully wrong. I've been divorced twice myself. I never kept it a secret."

"You're famous, Fee."

"I wouldn't have kept it a secret anyway. What was this Osborne? A beast? I'm sure there must be something."

"He has problems, Fee." What was the use of going into it now. God knows she had put it off for so long. Her secret, silent, other life. Although Brod was scrupulously polite she knew he had locked himself away from her.

How had she reacted?

She'd left with the freight plane while Brod, finding his own refuge, was staying out a full week at stock camp.

Rebecca shut off the word processor, sitting immobilised, lost in her thoughts. The book was good. It had taken on a real identity. At least she had given Fee that. The Kinross family, too. She had worked at a punishing pace. An act of atonement.

Brod!

Every time she thought of him she tried for her own survival to push his image away but her whole body remained pierced with longing and regret. She had fallen fathoms in love now the loneliness of it all. The febrile feeling in a body deprived of glorious sexual pleasure. No wonder she was so tightly strung up. But it hadn't hurt her work. In fact it gave a little credence to the old adage an artist had to suffer before inspiration flowed. If only Brod hadn't turned away from her. Not that she had given him much time, awash with her own bitter regrets.

For an instant Rebecca felt a sense of self-pity but she thrust it away. It was all her own fault. She had become entrapped in playing a certain role, adamant after Martyn her defences would never crumble. As a consequence she had paid the price.

Rebecca stood up determinedly. Enough writing for today. She needed a distraction. She really ought to go out and do a little shopping. It was Friday, the stores would be open until 9:00 p.m. She felt stiff from sitting too long in her chair. She placed her hands near the base of her spine, bending back gently, straightening up. She didn't have to look in a mirror to see how much weight she had lost. She could feel it. Very soon someone was going to mention the word anorexia but that wasn't her condition. She took care to eat the right things only sadness had shrunk her. She had always had chicken bones.

She decided to walk to the shopping village and get herself some smoked salmon, fresh fruit and vegetables. Some of those wonderful little rolls from the bakery, some dark rye bread for breakfast. Maybe a bottle of a good Riesling. It would keep for a couple of nights. She had to make a big effort to get back to normal. She had to be strong. It wasn't beyond her. She'd made a comeback after Martyn.

An image of Brod flashed before her eyes. Before grief flooded her.

Ally put her foot down and her small BMW accelerated smoothly, obedient to her touch. She'd been on location in tropical North Queensland for almost a month so many, many messages were waiting for her when she got home. One was from Fee to ring her, which she had immediately, listening as Fee told her all about the dramas that had been enacted at home.

"You're joking, Rebecca was once married?" Ally felt shocked, even a little outraged. "Why on earth didn't she tell us? I mean what was the big deal?"

"Obviously it was to Rebecca," Fee answered wryly. "Brod is terribly affected. He really loves her, darling. I'm sure of it."

"Well she mustn't love *him* if she can't confide in him," Ally countered sharply, then relented. "Heck who am I to judge? I've made a mess of my own life?"

"Do you think you can go and see Rebecca, darling?" Fee asked hopefully. "I can give you her address."

"Actually I've got it." Absently Ally turned up a page in her little black book. "That wouldn't be a problem, Fee. I suppose Brod's got very withdrawn?"

"I think he feels like murdering someone." Fee was driven to exaggeration. "You know Brod, darling. You know men."

"Not droves of them like you, dearest Fee."

"How naughty!" Fee wasn't offended. "I can't help thinking Rebecca is still hiding something."

"About her husband. Lord preserve us!"

"*Ex-husband* please, darling. He couldn't have been in jail. He works for James. Wait he's not with James any more. I suppose Brod had something to do with that."

"Did you ever think Rebecca might have experienced physical abuse in her marriage?" Ally wondered aloud.

"That little thing!" Fee's voice soared in shock. "Who would ever want to hurt such a beautiful little creature?"

"That's what I plan to find out."

When Ally reached Rebecca's block of flats she went to the floodlit entrance, let her gaze slide over the names and numbers. Hunt. R. Third floor, Unit 20. She found the buzzer, pushed it. No answer. She tried again. Damn, Rebecca wasn't at home. She should have rung first but she wanted the element of surprise. She had truly liked Rebecca from the moment she met her, a liking heightened by the knowledge her beloved brother had fallen deeply in love at last. Now Ally wanted to get to the bottom of what was keeping them apart. Was Rebecca a true enigma? A woman dangerous to love? Anything was possible.

Ally glanced at her watch, was about to move back to her car when she saw Rebecca walking down the road, a shopping bag in each hand. She looked as elegant as ever but Ally saw with concern she looked positively breakable.

"Rebecca!" Ally called brightly, waving a hand. She hurried forward to help with the parcels.

Rebecca came to a complete standstill, unexpected pleasure pouring into her. Ally was so emotionally strong. So vivid. "I thought you were away on your TV series?"

"All over." Ally flashed the radiant smile so well-known to her public. "Here, let me take one of those."

"Is everything okay?" Rebecca began, her face in the lamplight suddenly very pale.

"Lord, I've gone and frightened you," Ally said with quick understanding. "Everything's fine or as fine as it will be until you and I have a little talk. Tell you what, why don't you and I unload these and have a bite to eat somewhere. There must be dozens of restaurants around here."

"Why don't you let me make dinner," Rebecca offered. "I have a chicken, smoked salmon, all the ingredients for a salad. Fresh rolls. Even a good bottle of wine.''

"Lovely!" Ally said cheerfully. "I haven't had time for a bite to eat since breakfast. And I make a mean salad dressing. Paul Newman eat your heart out."

It was amazingly companionable. The best time Rebecca had had after the worst of times. Ally encouraged her to eat. "We're in no rush. I've nothing on." Her glance moved over Rebecca's petite frame. "You've turned positively fragile."

"Take a look at yourself then." Rebecca smiled.

"I eat all right—" Ally confirmed it by reheaping her plate "—but I'm on the run all the time. I haven't asked how the book is going?"

"I'm proud of it, Ally." Rebecca raised her eyes to Brod's sister's stunning face. So much like him. Except for the eyes, so perfectly like Fee's. "I know Fee is going to be very pleased with how it's turned out."

"We *all* will be," Ally corrected with a smile.

They cleared away first before they had coffee, taking it to the comfortable seating area in the combined living-dining room.

"You're a puzzle aren't you, Rebecca?" Ally said. "A puzzle I'm determined to solve. I adore my brother. When I came home for Dad's funeral I saw he was in love with you. I saw you returned his deep feelings."

"I love him," Rebecca admitted freely, "but there are so many things…"

"What things?" Ally set down her coffee cup. "Go on, explain. You can't close yourself in like a tomb. I'm here to help you, Rebecca. I'm not only Brod's sister, I'm your *friend*."

"I need one, Ally." Rebecca was very close to tears.

"Talk to me, girl." Ally leaned closer, her green gaze

compelling. "Tell me about that ex-husband you were forced to leave."

After about an hour the flood tide of words simply ran out.

"My God!" Ally breathed, rising to her feet and going to the balcony as if to get some fresh air. "What a monster!"

Rebecca caught her long hair and dragged it to the back of her head. "I thought I could never get over it until I met Brod."

"Brod!" Ally threw up her arms. "Brod could never behave like that to a woman. Never in a million light years." She shuddered at the very thought. "Why the man needs denouncing. And he had the hide to come after you. To set foot on Kimbara. I think Brod would kill him if he knew. No wonder you've found it so terribly difficult to speak. It must have been dreadful for you, Rebecca."

"Yes." Rebecca simply nodded, feeling strangely at peace and unburdened. "But I got away." She looked across the coffee table as Ally resumed her seat. "I think the image I wanted to present to the world was borne out of pain. Shame, too, I suppose."

Ally's vivid face looked saddened again. "And you didn't tell Brod because you thought he would think less of you. As though your husband's brutality had somehow infected you."

"That's it, exactly, Ally. Once I actually liked it when a male colleague told me I was like a white camellia. *Untouchable.* That was the image I wanted to project. Not a woman who had once crumpled under a man's hitting hands."

Ally's expression was very serious, even sombre.

"But you've won through, Rebecca. You've earned respect on all sides. It's that brute you were married to who was the coward. What you've told me makes my skin crawl."

"*You* wouldn't have put up with it, Ally."

Ally took a deep breath. "I had a family to call on, Rebecca. A very powerful family. Whatever my father's sins of omission he would never had stood by had I become involved in a disastrous marriage like that. Brod, well Brod, I wouldn't have liked to be the fella."

Rebecca nodded. "That's why I didn't tell him that night. I just couldn't start a terrible fight even if I did want Martyn thrown off the property."

"But you have to tell him now, Rebecca. You know that."

"I can't say to him what I've said to you, Ally. We're women. From what Fee told me Brod has already taken some action. Martyn's no longer with Matthesons."

"Great!" Ally applauded with a clap of her hands. "I think he might try another state. Western Australia wouldn't be far enough! Clear across the continent. Look, you've been working too hard. That's very clear to me. You need time off. A friend of mine has a gem of a beach house at Coff's Harbour. We could drive down tomorrow night. Spend a few days. What do you say?"

"To friendship." Rebecca raised her empty coffee cup, her eyes lighting up. "But what about you. You must have lots of things lined up?"

"I have, too, but I'd much rather go with you. You're going to come through this, Rebecca, or my name isn't Ally Kinross."

The weather was perfect. Glorious blue skies, marvellous surf. Ally's friend's little gem of a beach house

was big and fantastically beautiful, consisting of a series
of pavilions, some open air filled with wonderful Thai
furniture from Bangkok. Perched on the hillside over-
looking the Pacific Ocean, it had breathtakingly beautiful views and a long flight of steps that led down to
the white sandy beach. Even the sheltered front garden
was filled with beautiful things: palms, ferns, orchids,
water lilies and giant pots that lent a wonderfully exotic
touch.

In such an environment with Ally's company and the
healing powers of the blue sea and golden sun, Rebecca
began to relax. Ally was such a good and generous person Rebecca felt a deep gratitude for all her help.
Serious conversations punctuated the relaxation. Ally's
own love story came tumbling out. It was a warm, close
time. A time of getting to know each other properly.
By day they went for long walks along the beach,
swam, did a little sun-baking, explored the beautiful
coastline by car, visited all the little galleries and craft
shops, had al fresco lunches that turned into hours. They
stayed home at night making a meal, watching television, listening to music, before turning in, calm and
quiet.

It was on the Tuesday afternoon as Rebecca was re-
laxing in the open-air pavilion covered with its dark
timbered roof, Ally, looking marvellous in white shorts
that showed off her beautiful long legs and a little yellow top that left her golden midriff bare, came up the
stairs from the garden.

"Rebecca, love, we have a visitor," she called, a
decided lilt in her lovely voice.

"Really?" Rebecca swung her feet to the ground,
expecting to see the owner of this marvellous place.

Like Ally she was wearing beach clothes only her outfit was a beautiful sari she had bought at one of the local boutiques, its silky black background covered in brilliantly coloured tropical birds and flowers.

She waited a few seconds, receptive to whatever came, hearing the sound of footsteps coming up the stairs.

"My big surprise!" Ally announced as their visitor appeared, lifting herself up onto her toes to kiss her brother's lean, handsome cheek.

"Brod!" Rebecca drew in a sharp breath, the book she had been reading falling to the floor.

"Now I'm going to leave you two alone," Ally laughed. "I know you've got lots to talk about. I'm going down to the village. If Brod's going to stay we'll need more of everything." She turned jauntily, gave them a little wave. "Back in a hour or so you two."

While Rebecca stood rooted like some exotic flower, Brod walked towards her, taking his time, a quiet approach but his eyes were blazing over her.

"Hi!"

"Hi, yourself." It came out like a whisper and all because she was ecstatic to see him again. "Tell me how you got here?"

He put out his two hands and cupped her face. "Ally and I have the same friends."

"Oh!"

"By the way, you look beautiful."

"So do you."

"That's hard to believe."

They stood for a moment silent while Ally's BMW tore off accompanied by a loud honk of the horn.

"The only question is did you miss me?" He brought

her close to him and kissed her mouth. Tenderness and passion, the sweetest of wild honey.

Sensation swallowed her so she took a while to answer. "Never!" She shook her head at the same time, flashing him a luminous glance.

"The same for me," he teased. "I never thought of you once."

"You say the nicest things." There was an explosive excitement beneath the banter. He touched a little fold of material at her breast, indulging his senses in the satiny feel of her skin. "Well hardly at all," he amended, "except for the hours between one dawn and another. Night was the worst."

A feeling of intense joy rose in her. "For me, too. It's been a torture."

"When I think of what you had to suffer!" His voice was low and impassioned.

"Hush, it's all over." She raised herself on tiptoe, putting gentle fingers against his mouth, delighting in his little nipping kisses. "Ally told you?"

"Isn't that what sisters are for?" he asked gratefully. "Ally is amazingly intelligent and perceptive."

"You don't blame me?" She gazed intently into his eyes.

"Rebecca!" He held her questing glance for a long highly charged moment, the great surge of protectiveness he had experienced at the first sight of her, her femininity, her vulnerability, alchemising into pure passion. This was the woman he wanted with all his heart and soul. Nothing would have stopped him coming after her. With or without Ally. Abruptly he lowered his head covering her upturned face with kisses, then as her head fell back, the length of her neck. "You were right not to tell me about Osborne that night at the house. I think

I might have gone crazy had I known what he did to you. I can easily see now how you built up your defences and why. What we have to do now is burn them down.''

"When I'm already engulfed in fire." An answering moan of desire rose in her chest. "I love you, Brod. I adore you."

He felt an enormous surge of elation. "Are you absolutely sure of it?" He stared down into a pair of liquid diamond eyes.

"I'm going to die if you leave me," she said.

"My precious Rebecca!" He gathered her closely to him. "You deserve so much. I want to give it to you. Marry me."

Totally at peace, he began to kiss her again, moving his tongue against hers, exploring her mouth deeply, while sensation after sensation shot through Rebecca like little jolts of electricity. Down the length of her body, her limbs, her spine, between her legs.

"When is it Ally gets home?" he groaned against her mouth.

She whispered fluttery little endearments back. "An hour. Make it two. You know Ally."

"I do." He thought for a moment, then swept her up into his arms, causing another wave of sexual pleasure.

"Then we'll take it very...very...slowly," he said.

* * * * *

Look for Ally's story in
THE BRIDESMAID'S WEDDING
Coming soon from Margaret Way

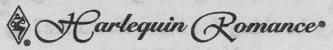
Harlequin Romance®

**On their very special day,
these brides and grooms are determined
the bride should wear white...
which means keeping passion in check!**

WHITE WEDDINGS

True love is worth waiting for...

Enjoy these brand-new stories from
your favorite authors

MATILDA'S WEDDING (HR #3601)
by **Betty Neels**
April 2000

THE FAITHFUL BRIDE
by **Rebecca Winters**
Coming in 2000

Available at your favorite retail outlet, only from

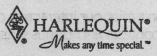
HARLEQUIN®
Makes any time special.™

Mother's Day is Around the Corner...
Give the gift that celebrates Life and Love!

Show Mom you care by presenting her with a one-year subscription to:

HARLEQUIN
WORLD'S BEST

Romances

For only $4.96—
That's **75% off the cover price.**

This easy-to-carry, compact magazine delivers 4 exciting romance stories by some of the very best romance authors in the world.

Plus each issue features personal moments with the authors, author biographies, a crossword puzzle and more...

A one-year subscription includes 6 issues full of love, romance and excitement to warm the heart.

To send a gift subscription, write the recipient's name and address on the coupon below, enclose a check for $4.96 and mail it today. In a few weeks, we will send you an acknowledgment letter and a special postcard so you can notify this lucky person that a fabulous gift is on the way!

Return to the charm of the Regency era with

GEORGETTE HEYER,

creator of the modern Regency genre.

Enjoy six romantic collector's editions with forewords by some of today's bestselling romance authors,

**Nora Roberts, Mary Jo Putney,
Jo Beverley, Mary Balogh,
Theresa Medeiros and Kasey Michaels.**

Frederica
On sale February 2000
The Nonesuch
On sale March 2000
The Convenient Marriage
On sale April 2000
Cousin Kate
On sale May 2000
The Talisman Ring
On sale June 2000
The Corinthian
On sale July 2000

Available at your favorite retail outlet.

HARLEQUIN®
Makes any time special ™